Honest Faces

Steven Donkin

Aberdeen Bay

Albion - Harbin - Topeka - Washington, D.C.

Aberdeen Bay
Published by Aberdeen Bay, an imprint of Champion Writers.
www.aberdeenbay.com

PUBLISHER'S NOTE

This is a book of fiction. Names, characters, places, and
incidents are either the product of author's imagination or are
used fictitiously. Any resemblance to actual persons, living or
dead, business establishments, government agencies, events,
or locales is entirely coincidental.

International Standard Book Number
ISBN-13: 978-1-60830-035-8
ISBN-10: 1-60830-035-8

Printed in the United States of America.

Acknowledgements

I want to thank my wife Julia Donkin for her unwavering patience and support throughout the writing of this little story, and for generously reading through and providing valuable criticism on several of its drafts. My thanks also go to Jenefer Ellingston for reading and commenting on an early draft, and to Jill Cline and Andy Zhang of Aberdeen Bay for accepting the final product for publication.

Honest Faces

PART I

CHAPTER ONE

The man, white-bearded, placidly eyeing the November drizzle from the cabin of the Newark-to-Pittsburgh jet as it held for take-off, felt the weight of age accumulating on his body like sediment. He, sixty-five years old, examined the faint, fleshy paleness of his face, nose slightly crooked, the bush-like aspect of his snowy hair and beard, superimposed upon the bleak rain-soaked scene presented through the tiny window. He saw also reflected, behind his own visage, the shaggy nape of the companion seated next to him, a young man who had already demonstrated an onerous loquaciousness, having slowly navigated his way to his seat while making embarrassing and unnecessary comments to fellow passengers, but who now through a stroke of luck was safely assaulting the passenger across the aisle with his vacuous chatter. The older man turned to ease back contentedly in his seat, into the long woolen coat he kept wrapped around his pallid, heavy bulk in case the cabin turned cold.

This much can easily be observed of him by way of introduction. For a more complete portrait, one must delve deep into his thoughts, running randomly yet with purposeful intent through his mind as they might through the mind of a seasoned thespian reviewing his major soliloquies for the opening night's performance.

Jonathan Allerton (he recited to himself), *on my way to visit my brother, Frank. I'm freshly retired from a respectable career in college professorship. Frank is ten years my senior. He and I grew up in a small town in eastern Ohio, raised by our widowed father, a man who did his best to juggle tending to our needs and running the town's only hardware store.*

He recalled that Frank, when he'd become old enough to sweep out the shop's stockroom, had found after-school and weekend employment with the father, gradually working his way up to driving the delivery truck, running the cash register, and negotiating with wholesale suppliers as his acumen developed. While Frank had shown little interest in schooling, Jonathan, for his part, had displayed a comparable dearth of enthusiasm for managing a hardware store. So it seemed natural that, when the father died suddenly just before Jonathan graduated high school, it would be Frank who stepped in to take full ownership of the business while Jonathan escaped to New Jersey, following the fortunes of a Princeton scholarship, then graduate school at Rutgers University and an eventual comfortable existence as an ivory tower academic.

The circumstances of their father's death, which had led to some bitter feelings between Frank and Jonathan, were these: one evening in late spring, nineteen sixty-one, Mr. Allerton collapsed while dragging a box of metal scrap across the stockroom floor after Frank had abandoned his shift early to drink in the tavern down the street with some college girls. Frank returned to the store four hours later and found his father unconscious on the cement floor, but he was so inebriated that it took him three attempts to place a coherent call to the paramedics. By the time they finally arrived, the old man was dead. They said they might have saved him had they been able to arrive sooner. He was buried a week later on a peaceful corner of the church cemetery where the new spring grass was lime-green, next to his wife who had preceded him in death by eleven years. After the funeral, an embittered Jonathan left home for college without saying goodbye to Frank, and the two brothers never spoke again. This much was the truth; this much was real.

The flight attendants were now performing their well-rehearsed safety routine. The captain came on the speaker for some last-minute words of reassurance, and the cabin sighed into placated silence. The plane slowly taxied up the runway, paused, turned ninety degrees, paused again, then started to move, accelerating with a howling whir of the engines. The white-bearded man closed his eyes as he felt the plane rush forward, tilt back, and ascend.

Frank will be waiting to pick me up at the other end, he thought. *What's it like, meeting someone you have neither seen nor spoken to for forty-seven years?* He pondered this, trying to see some unknown truth behind it. *A very long time. At least on a human scale.* Within forty-seven years, he knew, certain ties may be snapped and discarded, personal allegiances may dissolve and melt away; what one thought was settled may turn out to be only simmering; what was thought true may be revealed to be, well, less so.

The young verbal assailant in the next seat, having dispensed with his victim across the aisle, now inserted himself into the quiet thoughts of the white-bearded man peacefully dozing beside him. The older man was forced to defend himself by pretending he was hard of hearing, and quite possibly demented.

"Are you visiting family in Pittsburgh?"

"Huh? What's that? I couldn't hear you."

"I said are you visiting family in Pittsburgh?"

"Grandmother."

A confused pause followed. "Oh, uh, really?"

"She plays in the symphony. First oboe. Blows like an angel."

The young man stared, then looked worried, then turned his attention to a magazine in his lap and raised his eyebrows.

As the plane reached cruising altitude, the older man,

satisfied now, closed his eyes again and settled in for the flight. He felt the warmth of the coat around him, suffusing his body, displacing the last remnants of the icy chill that had accompanied him to the airport that morning. He listened to the calming engine drone, the scattered low conversations, the sounds of flight attendants readying the beverage server. The fluorescent interior lights dimmed. The murmur and hum of the cabin became distant. He was delightfully warm and at peace. *Will Frank know me? And I him?* He wondered at this as he drifted into sleep.

It was a quiet, deathlike sleep, timeless and directionless. Presently his mind fell into dreaming. He was in another place, away from the noises of the airplane, from the steel and hard plastic of the encapsulating cocoon. The setting of the dream which unfolded before him was familiar, although why he did not know. It appeared to be a sort of carnival on a lake shore at night. A hill descended gently to the shore, and down its slope was a long, wide path covered by a large black canvas that was supported by poles so the people could walk under it. And there were many people milling around, and the dreamer walked among them, although he recognized no one. On either side of the path, beneath the canvas, numerous tables and stalls displayed a large variety of wares, the substance of which he could not discern. And there were the lights—cavernous, unearthly lights. The length of the path was strung with many small illuminated bulbs attached to and hanging from the canvas ceiling. From the inside, the whole affair had a closed look, such as one might expect to find in a coal mine. On the outside, the slope was tiered with yet more pathways running transversely, also edged by various tables and stalls, unsheltered here by canvas but still illuminated with lights strung lengthwise between poles, like telephone lines. Everywhere the strange people were walking, chatting happily among themselves, looking at the items on the tables. Carefree, non-descript music filtered through the noise from somewhere in the distance. The dreamer still could not shake the feeling as he walked among the crowds that he had been here sometime before. He had an expectancy of meeting someone with whom he was acquainted, yet he had no idea who that person would be. It seemed an isolated, impossible place, like the apex of a great pyramid. He looked down the slope to the dark lake, its calm waters, and saw many small rowboats floating on its surface, with people barely visible in them, their silhouettes lit softly with candles lining the gunnels. The atmosphere all around was one of contented, naïve gaiety, but he alone felt an underlying current of menace.

As the dreamer slowly wended his way through the people down to the shore, he was suddenly overtaken by a couple, a man and a woman, running past him laughingly, hand-in-hand. He recognized the woman with a start when she turned her head to smile at the man, whose face was hidden in darkness. *My wife?* He called to her, "Ruth! Ruthie!", but she did not hear. He quickened his pace, following them, trying to catch up, but his progress was impeded by the other people, who jostled him and threw suspicious glances in his direction. When he finally reached the shore, the woman and man were gone. He searched frantically up and down the beach, to no avail. Standing at the water's edge, out of breath, trying to penetrate the darkness with his eyes, he noticed then that all sound had ceased, and he was suddenly, inexplicably alone. Behind him, he heard a low voice say, "They have taken a boat." He turned to see who had spoken, but no one was there.

The man awakened suddenly, finding himself still in the coach seat of the airplane, comfortably warm in his woolen overcoat. He noticed that, with the treachery that dreams play upon time, they were already making their descent into Pittsburgh. His neighbor, still absorbed in his magazine, made quick eye movements in his direction without turning his head, having been sufficiently deterred by their first encounter from attempting any further conversation. After landing with a jolt and a whine of the engines as the thrust reversers engaged, the plane crawled to the terminal gate and docked with assured calmness. The interior lights came on, passengers rose *en masse* from their seats like a well-trained regiment, and amid the bustle of retrieving luggage from the overhead bins, the two wary travelers exchanged polite smiles—one of which was overlaid with a measure of soft-eyed sympathy—and departed company.

Inside the terminal, dressed in jeans and a worn black parka lined with down, a small, wrinkled, sallow man stood, poised expectantly, with a look profoundly old and life-weary. He was intently scanning the emerging passengers with a thoughtful frown as they passed through the door. His eyes ran over the man in the long woolen coat with the bushy hair and white beard who had just come in, dismissed him, moved on to the others, then paused and returned to him, staring. His squinting eyes widened and his frowning expression relaxed into uncertainty as he spoke to the man now walking briskly toward him with a small brown leather valise in his hand. "Jonathan?" The bearded man grinned and nodded as he approached.

They shook hands awkwardly, a little nervously, the smaller man looking up at the other through thick, dusty plastic-rimmed glasses. "Well, my my my," he said, his face folding over itself like an accordion when he smiled. "You look good, Jonathan. I wouldn't have recognized you with all those whiskers." His own hair was white and quite thin on top; his clean-shaven face was book-ended by two overlarge ears which hung limply off the sides of his head.

"It's good to see you, Frank."

Frank was thoughtful for a moment, nodding, uncertain how to proceed. Then he quickly revived himself. "Do you have any luggage checked?"

"No no," came the reply, with a lift of the valise. "This is it."

They exited the airport, walking quickly and wordlessly through the cold, windy-gray parking lot to Frank's car. There was no rain here, only an overlying portent of somnolent dreariness. The weight of the long years between them made conversation difficult, and they both acknowledged this with strained silence as they got in the car and Frank started the engine. He drove around to the ticket booth and, paying the fee, exited toward the highway. It would be an hour or so drive back to Ohio and to Frank's house, plenty of time for unhurried talk. For now, the two passengers shivered against the lingering chill while the car's heater slowly kicked in. As they came upon Route 60 heading north, Jonathan looked around and took in the scenery, stark and drained of color. The sky was overcast and leaden. The last of the dead leaves had fallen from their trees; patches of frosted snow lay silent in shadowed ditches by the roadside.

"I really appreciate you driving out here to pick me up," Jonathan said. "I doubt that my car would have made it all the way from New Jersey."

Frank sucked in his breath before replying, to add emphasis. "Oh, no, it's no problem, Jonathan. I've got nothing but time, and I'm really okay driving as long as it's daytime."

The monotonous hum of the car's engine made a sorrowful soundtrack to the austere landscape moving past them. There were few other cars on the highway.

"So you've retired from the university?" Frank turned his head from the road and fixed his companion inquiringly, mouth open to half-smile and eyes enormous behind the magnifying lenses.

"Yes, as of August. Ruthie—the wife—still works at the stage designing outfit. They do sets for Broadway, some TV shows."

"Yes, yes. Oh my, that must be interesting." He returned his eyes to the road but nodded in the other's direction. He was really interested.

Jonathan shrugged. "Not really. She does the accounts. Gets a few tickets once in a while. It's all a little artificial to me."

"I see."

They drove further in thoughtful silence. The sky in front of them paled as the orb of the setting sun moved behind the clouds. A large hawk could be seen gracefully circling far above the woods to one side.

Frank spoke again. "And when was it you got married?"

"In, uh, seventy-three."

"Goddamn," he quietly exhaled. "I guess I missed—" He stopped himself, thinking about it, then said, with feigned cheer, "Well, look at me: lifetime bachelor, huh?"

"Yeah, well. . . "

"Each his own, I guess, right?" He turned and smiled. "What's she like? Any kids?"

"No. You, um, you gave up the store? Sold it?"

Frank stopped smiling. "Hmmm, yes. You'll see. Can't compete anymore with these big monster chains. It's the death of honest retail."

"That's tough."

They fell again into silence, each with his own thoughts. Frank was remembering his younger brother as a beardless, coal-eyed, board-solid eighteen-year-old. The old man sitting next to him now was white-haired, white-bearded and full-fleshed. How could time dispense such profound changes upon a human being? *But then*, he thought, *I've changed a lot too.* He wondered at how the other must see him, and remember him. *We really didn't recognize each other.*

Frank slowed the car, downshifting, easing onto the

exit ramp. They were beginning the second leg of the journey, accompanied by an unfolding of scenes that would include sullen, two-lane back roads pushing up against tall dead grasses skirted with snow, remote forests of dormant trees, gas stations and food stores with drab gravel parking lots. They drove several miles in this fashion, still without speaking. *He's taking it all in,* Frank thought. *He hasn't been here in forty-seven years and it's a lot to take in.* Frank watched his passenger through the corner of his eye when they pulled up to a stop sign. He was looking out his window, expressionless. *What's he thinking?* Frank wondered.

And now as they turn the corner and begin a winding tree-lined ascent up a somber, gradual hill, it is the past catching up, rushing up to the present, to finally overtake it and carry it forward, that hits them both like a sea wave.

"Hasn't really changed much, huh, Jonathan?" Behind the trees, the yellowish-brown remnants of harvested hayfields are visible. "Mr. and Mrs. Clayburn died of course." He nods toward a two-level farmhouse to the left. "Kids sold the place, moved off. Cecil—you remember Cecil—killed in a car wreck on this road ten years ago. He was an accident waiting to happen. They shut down the textile mill in the seventies—that's just empty buildings now. Lotta people left—or died. Few new ones come in, but no young people. 'Cept little Cora's got a niece from Cincinnati living with her. Fine young lady. Schoolteacher. Downtown's pretty much the same, but a lot of businesses got hurt when the mall come in. Most people go out there to do their shopping."

As he speaks, his passenger surveys his surroundings, interjecting an occasional monosyllabic to indicate he is listening. The road straightens and they pass a low, sprawling brick building surrounded by parking lot and manicured grass. Beside it is an unseasonably green field with large yellow padded goal posts at each end, surrounded by a running track, with empty aluminum bleachers rising at the sides, all enclosed by a shabby and well-worn chain-link fence. Outside of the fence, adjacent to it, is a grassless open area with rusted iron goal posts, blotched with patches of brown dirt and snow.

Frank is saying, "High school got a new football field. We used to play on the older field. Don't know if you remember that?" He turned inquiringly.

"Barely."

They finally come upon a section of road populated by a number of evenly spaced one-story houses with small yards. The western sky now glows a soft pink, the sun sinking, settling in behind the black trees. They turn into the driveway of a white rectangular house with a sagging porch and gray shutters on the windows. It is slightly warmer now, a short burst of pre-dusk sunshine having melted the remaining snow from the yards and driven off the afternoon chill. A stooped middle-aged woman in a pink and white quilted housecoat stands at the far end of the neighbor's yard, gripping the handle of a rake, staring down at a small pile of leaves. She has messy black hair and black cat eye glasses. She is unmoving, as if time had momentarily halted.

Climbing out of the car with a groan, Frank said, "That's my neighbor Ruth," nodding in the woman's direction. "Same name as your wife." He smiled up at Jonathan with raised eyebrows, expecting surprise.

"How 'bout that."

"She lives with her father—retired army colonel." He called to her. "Hello, Ruth!"

The woman looked up from her leaf pile, maintained the grip on the rake, and squinted. Then she smiled broadly. "Hi, Frank!" Her smile was bucktoothed and full of saliva. "I found a snake in the cellar this morning but I killed it with a shovel!" She smiled again.

"My, that's fine. Uh, Ruth, this is my little brother Jonathan from New Jersey." He held his hand out to his side, open-palmed.

Jonathan waved. "Hello, Ruth. My wife's name is Ruth too."

"I'm not married yet," she shouted back irrelevantly.

With keys in hand, Frank mounted his porch, unlocked the door, entered and flipped the light switch. Jonathan followed, setting his valise on the floor. He noted that the house had a large square front room, with a hallway to the kitchen in the back. The two bedrooms were on opposite sides of the hall, the bath next to Frank's room and a small study adjacent to the guest room.

Frank said, "I'll fix us some tea—and some supper if you like."

"Fine. Do you need any help?"

"No no. Just make yourself at home there." He hung his parka on a nearby coat rack and shuffled down the hall to the kitchen, floorboards creaking beneath his footfalls. The sounds of clanging metal pots soon echoed from the back of the house. Jonathan heard the furnace in the basement switch on, blowing heated air out of the floor vents. He stood in the center of the front room, removed his woolen coat and hung it up, then scrutinized his surroundings with a museum patron's interest.

The walls were a milky tan color, with a few framed prints of watercolor woodland scenes, no portraits or family photographs. A small brown bookcase stood against one wall, and on top of it was set a lamp with a lathed cherrywood base and an orange shade. Next to the lamp sat an old-style radio receiver with a chrome dial and two tiny speakers. Some dusty hardbound books leaned wearily on the lower shelves. A small television on an aluminum cart, a rocking chair in the corner, and a claret-colored sofa on top of a blue woven rug in the center of the room completed the picture.

The tea kettle whistled from the kitchen. Jonathan heard the sounds of silverware being set, smelled the steak and potatoes frying. "I hope you're hungry, Jonathan," Frank called, a tinny echo in his voice.

"Sure." The silence in the house was disquieting to him, but he could see Frank was comfortable in it.

Supper was served under the long fluorescent ceiling light in the kitchen. The curtainless window above the sink was dark and empty, as if there was nothing beyond. They ate in silence at first, drinking tea out of chipped porcelain cups. Jonathan noticed that Frank liberally sprinkled his with cheap bottom-shelf bourbon, declined an offer to do the same.

Frank spoke first. "Fella next door," he nodded over his shoulder to indicate the direction, chewing, "Conrad the Colonel—we usually have a little get-together there Friday nights. Sit around drinking, discussing world affairs. Sometimes we play a little five-card stud, low stakes, nothin' serious. Would you like to go tomorrow night?" He looked up at Jonathan pleasantly.

The other nodded, swallowed a gulp of peas. "Sure."

"Give you a chance to see some of the local folk." He paused, chewing, staring at the table in front of him. "I don't guess Conrad and Ruth were here when you left. Or maybe you just hadn't met them. He'd been out of the country a lot. Military, y'know. The family was already next door when I moved into this house; that's when I moved away from Dad's—" He paused again, threw an uncertain glance at a trashcan in the corner. Shrugging, he went on. "Malcolm Peters may stop by too. Colored fella, but nice as hell. Retired teacher, moved here a couple years ago. A widower."

"Sounds fine." A silence.

Frank lowered his eyebrows, looking down at the table again. "When I first heard from you, Jonathan, and you said you were comin' to visit, I admit I was quite surprised. Seein' as

we hadn't really seen each other or even talked in. . . since—"
He looked up at the other across the table, as an apparent
prelude to asking a question, but he simply said, "It is nice to
see you, Jonathan." Their eyes held each other silently for a
moment longer, a moment occupying dimensionless space and
an unbounded, metricless time. Then Frank lowered his head,
pushed back his chair, and stood up. He collected the silverware
and empty plates and walked toward the sink.

Jonathan called to him over the sound of running water.
"You're wondering why, after all these years, I decided to come
back. It's a good question. I can't say I know the answer exactly
myself. We both know we've never been close." A pause. "I,
um, I guess with my retirement I found that certain things
gnawed at me. Certain unknowns. Mainly about myself, but
also about us."

Frank returned to the table, collected the drained teacups.
"It's okay, Jonathan," he said without looking up. "You don't
have to explain yourself. I'm just glad you came."

They left the kitchen and Frank turned out the light. It
was fully dark now. Jonathan retrieved his valise from the front
room, and Frank led him to the guest room, where he laid the
valise on the bed.

Frank said, "I s'pose you're somewhat fatigued from
your trip. I go to bed early myself. I like to watch a little TV
before turning in. You're welcome to join me."

"No, I guess I'll just unwind in here."

"All right. Towels and things are in the bathroom across
the hall. Help yourself."

As he turned to leave, Jonathan called after him,
"Frank?" Frank paused, looked around. "I'd really like to visit
some of the old places while I'm here, Frank. The old house, the
store."

Frank regarded the other with a sad, indulgent smile.
"Oh, yes. Yes, Jonathan, we can do that."

He left the room, closing the door behind him.

Sitting on the bed now in the quiet of the guest room, the reading lamp lit on the white marble top of the nightstand, staring at the red electric numerals on the clock-radio, Jonathan, becalmed and reflective, parts his lips and inhales. He looks down at his shoes, heavy boots really, heavy and dull black and thick-soled, and at the thick knotted pine planks of the flooring, yellow and rubbed smooth by the soles of countless shoes like his. He exhales slowly, turns his gaze to the open valise beside him on the bed.

"Well." He stares, breathing easily. The faint sound of the television filters in from the front room.

I should call Ruth, he thinks. *I should let her know I made it.* He reaches for the valise and pulls out a cell phone. She should be at home now. He punches in the numbers of the house.

After four rings he hears her voice on the answering machine. He looks at the clock-radio again. *9:30.* She wouldn't be in bed yet. After the beep he speaks into the phone: "Hi, it's me. Just wanted to let you know I'm here. Everything's okay. Bye."

He closes the phone, sits there for a moment, thinking, trying to remember something just beyond the boundary of memory. "Well." He looks at the closed door to the hallway for a moment, sees his reflection in the full-length mirror hanging on the door, the look of puzzlement in his face. Then he exhales loudly again, turns to remove the valise from the bed, place it on the floor and pull back the red coverlet. With weary heaviness, he undresses.

CHAPTER TWO

He lay in the darkened room, staring up at the whitish ceiling, which was altered to a bluish tinge by the light of night, the mist-suffused blue-black light creeping softly through the lace-curtained window. He heard rain falling outside, softly, like diaphanous fabric settling itself, layer by layer, upon the earth. The last of the snow would be washed away by morning.

What was Ruth doing right now? he wondered. *Where is she?*

Ruth wouldn't have wanted to come here, he knew. She disliked the unassuming quietude of small town life, preferring instead the anonymous frenzy of the urban beehive. She had no desire to relinquish it, having finally staked her small claim on it after a lifetime of pursuit. *A lifetime of pursuit*, he thought, remembering.

Closing his eyes now, his mind wandered through the past to a dreary backlit third-floor apartment on the north side of New Brunswick one dismal winter afternoon forty years ago. They were college students then, she an undergraduate in business accounting, he in pursuit of his doctorate in chemistry. And in the background, as so often it was, he remembered, the room imbued on this day with the ethereal loveliness of guitar music straining through the phonograph speakers: John Fahey, "On the Sunny Side of the Ocean." It was the kind of transcending, yearning anthem that was capable of lifting him beyond the bleak New Jersey squalor surrounding him. *Why does music stir the emotions so?* he'd wondered that day.

It's effects were primal, arousing, even akin to sexual ecstasy, with the right piece, with particular chord changes or certain harmonic nuances. The apartment was small and colored in black, gray and white. He remembered Ruth as she lay naked but modestly covered under the quilts on the fold-out sofa he used for a bed. She was listening passively to the music with eyes closed. He was casting glances at her as he hurriedly flipped through chemistry textbooks piled haphazardly on the floor, moving quickly because he was also naked, pale and uncovered. The muffled sounds of car traffic and rainy drizzle filtered through the closed blinds, over the sofa-bed, and mingled with the melodic arpeggios swelling against the walls.

"You'll get chilled walking around the cold room like that," she murmured without opening her eyes.

"I'm looking for something a business major wouldn't appreciate," he replied with another glance in her direction, an attempted smile, though she did not see it.

"This business major at least understands the physics of heat enough to know you'd better get under the covers before you freeze."

She rolled on her side and propped herself up on one elbow, lifting the quilt, demurely but very deliberately exposing her breasts in the muted light, fixing him with a hard stare and a savage, inviting smile.

"All right," he said, shrugging. "Fourier will just have to wait."

He tumbled onto the mattress and commenced to take in her warm body, sliding his palms over her skin, nuzzling her with his lips and nose, and they giggled and made love with obdurate sincerity until the room darkened into dusk long after the despondent guitar music had stopped. He remembered that day now, particularly, at that moment, though he did not know why.

They had been a tenuous couple for three months by then, and had had many such afternoons together. She was to finish her degree long before he was to defend his dissertation. Their moments together were measured in short, desperate hours spent within the confines of that cramped apartment, with incidental music from lonely, hopeful, desolation-filled folk songs playing on the stereo: Odetta, Victor Jara, Phil Ochs, Bert Jansch, and, of course, Fahey, all drifting through varying moods of despair and longing.

This waking dream, he recalled, was often like a play in which actors exchange roles without warning. There was Ruth and Jonathan, and a character named Jake Reese Hart, an oddly empathetic fellow traveler in the university's graduate chemistry department. Jake was brilliant, understated, enigmatic, and more than casually engaged by the human condition. He saw himself as a suffering prophet, even a ministering overseer of the sorrow that binds us one to another. Jake was a Buddhist, or so he advertised himself. He aspired to be a healer of sorts.

"Tell me what's wrong," he would say to Jonathan late at night in the Raman spectroscopy lab, when the latter felt like keeping his thoughts to himself. "You're troubled, aren't you?" he'd ask.

"Why do you assume as much?" Jonathan would reply, not looking up from a newly printed absorption spectrum.

"Your vibe," he'd say, and, strangely, he'd be right.

Jake was Jonathan's age, fair and rough-hewn in appearance like Jonathan, with obsidian-black eyes, severe in demeanor, also like Jonathan, yet with a passionate intensity that Jonathan had to admit he could never cultivate in himself.

"We're really not that different from each other, Jonathan," he'd say. That too he had to acknowledge, although he always felt a momentary prick of panicked jealousy when Jake would voice the same sentiment to Ruth. "We're like two peas in a pod, me and Jonathan," he told her once when the three sat around a corner table at Victor's feasting on pizza and beer one snowy Saturday evening. Jonathan looked out the window at the empty, white-powdered lamplit streetscape and probably thought, yes, Jake, you're right.

Even after the marriage, when Ruth had a starting position at her cousin's stage design company in Jersey City, they still made regular excursions together into New York on the PATH train. They'd go to Greenwich Village to see live music, shop in the used book stores, see an occasional film that Jake had selected. They went to the premiere of "Last Tango in Paris," and Jake commented that a sexual relationship based on mutual anonymity was the preferred human condition. "Aren't we all anonymous to each other after all?" he'd said. Ruth nodded in agreement. When they saw Bergman's "Persona," Jake sat in rapturous enthrallment, eyes staring and mouth open, while Jonathan dozed with Ruth's hand in his lap.

And now he began dozing in the bed, these memories retreating in his mind. The gentle sound of rain outside his window had ceased. He imagined now that he heard the wind picking up, bringing in another cold front, and the distant cry of a train whistle. Maybe he'd heard these things, and maybe he'd begun to dream, presently falling into deeper sleep, though he would not quite recall it in the morning, having only a lingering notion, an almost extra-perceptual sense, that he'd again journeyed to the carnival on the lake shore.

CHAPTER THREE

The last star of dawn burned cold, distant and silent in the western sky. Across the great black dome, clouds retreated to make room for the rising sun, having been pushed eastward by a cold front moving down from the great lake far to the north. He moved his gaze from the sky to the barely visible yard below him, slowly emerging in the lavender stillness.

"Come, Maggie."

It was quiet in the yard except for the few harried clucks of the chickens, scattered by the lumbering Labrador retriever's half-hearted feints of pursuit. Flatly described, the dog was old, black, and going gray around the muzzle. *Just like her owner,* Malcolm Peters mused, smiling. *But she has a good soul — also, I hope, like me.* He clapped his hands together.

"Come on now. Let's go in." His breath was vaporous in the cold air.

The dog ran past him and up the wooden steps to the back door, tail wagging. He opened the door and they both went in.

The radio was on in the kitchen, tuned to the morning news: stories about the banking crisis, corporate failures, war, and the recent election.

The election. He thought about that as he prepared breakfast: a can of dog food for Maggie and some fried eggs and toast for himself. It made one hopeful, he reflected; it made one almost optimistic, like recovering from a disease that had been thought fatal. And hope itself was not a thing to be trivialized. It had turned many lives in compassionate, productive directions, filled them with purpose and drive. This he had observed himself.

Still, I wish Anna could have seen it. She'd have been so proud, so joyful. He paused for a moment, thoughtful, then sighed. "Tommy now," he said aloud, addressing the dog, "I'm glad he's seen it in his lifetime, but he's younger generation. He can't really feel it like us older folk, what with all we've lived through, y'know?" He turned to look at Maggie, who tilted her head to one side as she stared up questioningly at her master.

"Here y'go." He placed the dog's bowl, piled high with moist meat, on the floor and stepped back to watch her devour it with gusto.

The radio was saying that the day would be sunny, clear and very cold. He toasted some wheat bread in the oven, flipped the eggs in the frying pan with a crackle of fragrant grease. His nostrils flared at the odor as he turned up the radio. The President-elect was making choices for his administration already, they said. There was also an announcement that a local church was soliciting food donations for Thanksgiving gift baskets to feed the disadvantaged. Malcolm checked the cabinet and made a mental note to buy more coffee filters as he pulled down the last one. A small ray of golden light brightened the room as the sun peeked over the horizon, shone through the window and onto the vinyl flooring in front of the stove. He looked down. *Better mop today.*

Removing the sizzling pan from the fire, he deposited the eggs onto a plate, then retrieved the toast and carried the plate and a freshly poured mug of coffee to the small table, setting them in place with care. Satisfied, he wiped his hands on the flanks of his dungarees and sat down. Maggie concluded her feast with a prolonged licking of the chops, followed by a sloppy lapping at her water bowl. Malcolm picked up the local newspaper, delivered yesterday. It was no *Washington Post*, he knew, but he was getting used to wading through the small-town news to get at the national stories that really interested him. And he assiduously avoided the editorial columns. Reading silently, he ate slowly, lifting the fork to his mouth without taking his eyes from the page.

He finished his breakfast and pushed back the chair to get up. "Go lay down, Maggie." He sensed the dog wagging her tail expectantly behind him. "You've already had yours." She obediently turned and wandered into the living room. Malcolm walked to the sink, placed the dishes in the soapy water, and looked up at the yard, now sunlit and fully visible through the window. Behind his house, past the chicken pen, a wooded area thick with bare trees and evergreens screened his property from the dormant field beyond. A shallow creek coursed among these trees like a gurgling capillary, hidden deep within a gully several feet below the level of the ground. Along its edge there ran a well-worn footpath, a shortcut between the houses to the south and the elementary and high schools to the north.

A young woman wearing a long dark coat, black knit woolen hat pulled over her ears, and a long black scarf tucked snug around her collar trudged briskly along the path toward the north. She was slightly hunched, purposeful in her gait, with a large black backpack apparently weighing her down some. Her breath appeared in quick white puffs.

There she goes, he thought. *Fisher of young minds.*

It hadn't been too long ago that he was a similar sort of missionary, or so he'd believed at the time. That was in another place, a city, and the minds were of another ilk too. Troubled, angry, ill-nurtured minds often. Difficult to manage, let alone mold into educated, responsible citizenry.

Well, who's to say she doesn't face the same here? Children are children. They all need fostering; they need guidance and care. But he knew the contingencies of life play cruelly with the fates, sometimes at least. Everyone doesn't always get what he needs, or deserves. He turned from the window and switched off the radio. *I hope she can do better with her charges than I did with mine,* he concluded with finality.

He focused his mind on the day's tasks ahead: some shopping errands to run, chores around the house, and finally a social evening at the Colonel's house. He didn't mind these occasional bull sessions with the Colonel, Frank and whomever else might drop in. They weren't bad folk, most of the locals. Just a little, well, different from what he was used to. *I guess I'm different from what they're used to as well,* he thought, with some seriousness.

In any case, he considered, it could be a late evening. "I'd better set aside time this afternoon for a nap."

CHAPTER FOUR

On Friday morning, Frank awoke early as usual, the stillness of the pre-dawn darkness in his room feeling subtly altered and fragmented compared with the comfortable familiarity of previous mornings. Aided by the faint glow of the nightlight in the corner outlet, he reached to the nightstand for his glasses and was reminded of the change to his now-focused surroundings. There was another in his house, a mysterious stranger who brought with him memories that might just as well have been forgotten, that stirred emotions and dredged regrets that Frank had long ago buried. *I'm seventy-five years old*, he said to himself. *I don't need any more reminders of my past.*

He recalled the letter he received several weeks ago to which he did not respond. It appeared to be a plea to make things right between them as brothers. Jonathan apparently wanted to lay the past aside and have the brothers be reconciled again. After all, blood relations they were, and so they would always be.

I should do something. I should even the score in his favor. He's my only brother. Even after forty-seven years, he is still my brother and I must look out for him. I have no other kin.

And yet, it didn't feel right. So many years, so many cycles of seasons had passed. He had seen so many long winters like the one just now coming upon them; they seemed endless and final in their dreariness, unrelentingly solid in their coldness, their absence of respite.

Frank wondered as he rose from the bed how, within

the boundaries placed upon him, he could hope to correct his past transgressions in his relationship with the absent brother. He had left the letter unanswered, pondering the possibilities. And then the unexpected phone call, followed by the actual visit—these added another urgent dimension to his dilemma. There was now only one way he could imagine to move forward and make peace with his own conscience. But that would have to wait a day or two.

He opened the bedroom door and turned down the hallway to the kitchen, where he found his visitor already dressed and seated at the table with a newspaper in front of him, placidly staring out the curtainless window. He turned as Frank entered. "Good morning," he greeted his host. "Big day today. I'm anticipating an illuminating stroll down memory lane with you, Frank."

"Yes, well, we'll see what we can do, Jonathan." He was avoiding eye contact. "Remember, a lot's changed."

"Oh, certainly. But one thing that hasn't changed is that we're brothers. And we're the only family we've got, right? I want you to know, Frank, that I'll always be there for you. We can't let our foolish behavior in the past toward each other get in the way of our future. I want to turn over a new leaf, as it were."

Frank gave a relieved smile and now met the other's gaze. "I appreciate that. I feel the same way." He began to busy himself with the coffeemaker at the counter. "Tell me about your wife, Jonathan," he called over his shoulder as he worked. "Is she much like you?"

"Oh, very much so. When I spoke to her on the phone last night she was lying in bed reading one of her romance novels. A real homebody."

"I'd like to meet her sometime." Hearing no reply, he turned with an expectant smile, saw that his brother was staring off distractedly into the hallway.

"Hmm?" He looked up suddenly. "Oh, yes. We'll see if that can be arranged."

He rose from his seat and started to walk out, leaving the newspaper on the table. "They say it's going to be cold today," he said, as if his mind was elsewhere. "I'd better go dig out a warmer shirt."

He left the room, with Frank looking after him. The sun was beginning to brighten the sharp, cloudless sky, rising low in the east. Frank turned to squint out the window, looking far to the distance for some reassurance that the day would go well. Not finding any, he attempted an indifferent shrug, unconvincingly, and returned to preparing the coffee.

CHAPTER FIVE

"I hope you're not disappointed, Jonathan," Frank was saying. "Disappointed in me. In. . . well—" He spread his arms as they both stood on the edge of the vacant lot in the cold noon sunshine later that day. Frank's car was parked nearby on a pebble-strewn driveway.

They were looking, standing together and looking across the brightly lit field of dead grass and overgrown weeds. Above, the sky was a stark blue, as clear as a church bell's peal. A tall, wide, leafless chestnut tree spread out about thirty yards in front of them. Beyond that were the remains of a square, brown brick and masonry block foundation, now crumbled and decayed. The footprint of the house had been large, one could see that. The dugout cellar had been partially filled in with dirt and trash; there were remnants of oak floorboard scattered about on top of the fill. The only other clue that this had once been a house was an ornately balustraded oak staircase, charred black, rising about six feet, then suddenly ending in midair, with a partial wall attached.

He had sensed a reluctant tenseness in Frank that morning, when the idea of a visit to the old house came up again. Jonathan had slept poorly; despite being nestled in the warm sturdy comfort of Frank's guestroom, he was beset with nightmarish sensations brought on perhaps by the rising ghoulish howl outside his window, or by his own inner visions of disquietude. He could remember no specifics of any dream he may have had, only the vague feeling of floating high in the star-pointed, black stratosphere, looking down at civilization far below, with a coldness of feeling more stone-like than death. When he woke from his uneasy slumber before the sun came up, he had to lie in bed for a long while in order to gather together his dissipated energy. Now in the bright gleam of cold day, with the vertical sunshine banishing all shadow from the scene before them, the terrors of the night before seemed distant and otherworldly.

"What happened?" Jonathan's voice was barely audible, despite the ambient silence.

"It burned twenty-five years ago." They both wore heavy overcoats, but Frank was still shivering. A slight breeze came up and played with the silver strands on his hatless head. "I, uh, I wasn't home at the time. They said it was an electrical fault in the wall. When I got here, the fire department was just letting it burn. It was so fast, there was nothing they could do. Everything was gone."

Thoughts of rage and pity congealed into a vile soup in the other's brain. He continued to stare at the ruin. He was having difficulty believing it. He saw now why his cajoling over breakfast had appeared to produce an unexplained apprehension in Frank. "Yes, Jonathan," Frank had said, with a surprising lack of enthusiasm. "We can go see the old haunts. But what's the rush?" Now it was clear what he meant.

Frank was speaking again. "It was such a beautiful house. Two stories. And that big attic that ran the whole length of it. You used to love going up there and hiding out. Remember, Jonathan?"

"Frank."

"And the yard seemed so big to us when we were kids. Of course now it don't seem so, but it sure was a lot to maintain when I took it over—"

"Frank," he interrupted, still looking ahead. "There was—some money. . . "

Frank looked at him. "Oh, uh, yes. You remember that? Dad was afraid to keep money in the bank, ghosts of the Depression and all. He always set aside some ready cash, in the metal box behind the wall in his bedroom. He showed it to me. Said it would be ours when he passed on. 'Course you up and left, said you weren't interested. . . " He tried to meet the other's eyes.

But Jonathan continued to stare straight ahead. "What happened to it?" he asked feebly. "You didn't keep it in the house, did you?"

Frank looked at the ground. "Gone." He continued to shiver. "The box couldn't take the heat of the fire."

"You kept it in the house? All that cash?" His voice was a whisper, carried away instantly in the cold breeze. "How much?"

"Well, I, uh, you know, I added some to it occasionally, just like he did. And I was very good about not taking much from it, except for emergencies." He raised his eyes and exhaled, blowing a white puff of steam through his lips. "It was just over sixty-thousand."

For the first time Jonathan turned to face him, but slowly, with something less than emotion. He noticed that Frank's ears and nose were red with the cold.

Reading something in Jonathan's expressionless face that unsettled him, Frank was quick to continue, the words spilling over themselves as he spoke. "Now don't get angry, Jonathan. Please. Lord knows I've suffered for it. But you never cared about the money anyway. You said you didn't need it and didn't want it. I. . . I guess you were angry about Dad. . . about me—"

"Why didn't you put it in a bank?" Jonathan's voice was steely, distant.

"Well, now, I don't know. Y'know, Dad never trusted banks and—" he laughed a little uncomfortably,"—well, banks today aren't even that safe, are they?"

"It's not the Great Depression, Frank." He sighed loudly, faced forward again. "You could've just kept it in a safe deposit box. Why keep something like that in a hundred-year-old wooden house?" He paused, inhaled, calming himself. "Was it insured?"

"Not the money, no. It was all undeclared. Uncle Sam didn't know about it." He took a handkerchief out of his coat pocket and rubbed his nose, then sniffed. "The insurance money from the house was helpful in getting me the place I live in now, getting me settled there. I had to stay with Orrin and Brenda for quite a while, waiting for things to come together. You remember them. They—"

"Frank. It's not just the money. It—I mean, yes, it is the money." He turned his head and looked at Frank. He thought, then relaxed his expression. The brightness of the day was making him squint now, or perhaps it was a slight smile that gently creased the skin around his eyes. "It's not about the money, Frank," he said softly. "But what do you have to live on now? Social Security? Do you have anything from the store?"

"A little bit, yes. Oh, I'm fine. I don't need much. And you know," he smiled weakly, "us old folk don't have much longer anyway."

Jonathan continued to stare at him with an expression Frank could not decipher. He forced his breath steadily, deliberately through his nose. "So you've got. . . nothing?"

Frank looked away again, to the place where the house used to be. "I've got what I need, yes."

They stood in silence for a minute, each not looking at the other. Finally, Frank said, reluctantly, "I know my life has been one fool thing after another. I know that. And I know I've disappointed people, and hurt people. I never intended to. It just seemed to happen. And now I'm. . . I'm just not any use to anyone." Silence. The distant rumble of a freight train drifted

over the woods from beyond the vacant field. Frank looked up
at his companion. "Jonathan?"

He did not answer. He was staring straight ahead,
squinting, thinking. This maudlin display of self-reproach
was not to his liking. Could all the regret and self-pity in the
world make up for the damage people do to one another? The
perpetual abrogation of responsibility? He was thinking now,
recalling the dream from the previous day on the airplane, with
its lingering air of malfeasance, of a terrible wrong having been
committed. *I have seen this before*, he thought. *Why be surprised
now?*

Frank was talking, his eyes pleading, craving a response
of any kind. "Jonathan, I hope it doesn't matter much to you.
Used to be if someone threw a dollar bill on the ground you
couldn't even be bothered to pick it up."

He continued to look forward, speaking into the wind.
"You knew me a long time ago, Frank. Things change. People
change." Then after a moment he exhaled conclusively, shoved
his hands deep into his coat pockets and turned to Frank with a
grin. "But what's done is done, right Frank-o?"

His suddenly insouciant manner caught Frank unawares,
leaving him little choice but to reply with a smile and shrug,
"Yeah, I s'pose."

Jonathan turned and started back to the car. "How about
a walk through downtown, Frank? You up for it?"

Revitalized, Frank trotted up behind him, saying
cheerfully, "Sure. That's a good idea."

CHAPTER SIX

Frank pulled open the screen door under the single burning porch bulb and rapped loudly with his bare knuckles on the inner door, then immediately began rubbing his hands together and blowing into them. "Damn, it got cold again fast." He stamped his feet on the boards beneath him and grinned up at Jonathan. "Now, Conrad can be generous to a fault, but he's just 'bout the orneriest sumbitch you ever—hey, Ruth!" He turned suddenly as the door swung open and the woman with the cat eye glasses appeared. Quickly leaning in, he said conspiratorially, "Where's your dad?"

Wearing a broad, toothy smile and the same dowdy housecoat she'd been seen in the day before, Ruth stepped aside to let the two men enter, her eyes downcast, never meeting theirs. As they passed, Jonathan said softly, "Hello, Ruth," removed his hat. She said nothing, merely nodded and smiled at the floor.

"Shut the goddamn door, Frank!" a voice from inside bellowed loudly, but without malice. "My heat bill's through the roof." Continuing in, as Ruth took their coats and hats, they could see now under an archway at the far end of the front room a taut, solid, glaring old man in a wheelchair, wearing a button-down blue-green flannel shirt with sleeves rolled up to the elbows, revealing wire-haired forearms hardened with the grip he maintained on the chair's wheels. His hair was a freshly-mowed carpet of white bristles, below which sloped a broad forehead supported by two furry white caterpillar eyebrows shading intense blue eyes. The room stank of cigar smoke. The man in the wheelchair held the smoldering offender delicately between the index and middle fingers of his left hand, deftly maneuvering the chair with his remaining six fingers and two thumbs to face the new arrivals.

Frank said, "Evening, Conrad." He turned to indicate his companion. "This is—"

"No, let me do it!" Ruth interrupted, smiling excitedly. She took a deep breath and said, "Dad, this is Frank's little brother from New Jersey." She stood back on her heels, satisfied, knitting her fingers together in front of her.

Jonathan walked to the man and extended a hand. "Jonathan. Flew in yesterday. Frank picked me up in Pittsburgh."

The man in the wheelchair took the offered hand, gripped it firmly, looking up and examining the other with concentrated attention. "Conrad Haygood, U.S. Army, retired. Everyone but your brother here calls me Colonel." He scrutinized his guest for a moment longer, then released his hand and transferred the burning cigar stub from left to right.

"You're dropping ashes on the floor!" Ruth scolded with overblown passion.

"You're gonna vacuum tomorrow anyways, aren't ya?" he retorted angrily, shoving the cigar in his mouth so as to free his hands and grip hard the wheels of his chair. He directed himself toward the adjoining room.

"What's under the bar tonight, Conrad?" Frank asked, following.

The Colonel turned his head. "What? Oh, yeah. Come on in." He propelled himself under the archway into a dining room furnished in dark oak, in the center of which was an elongate table bracketed by matching high-backed chairs. There was a heavily cushioned chair in the corner and a tall sideboard topped with various bottles of liquor and mixers, tumblers, and a bucket of ice.

"Jonathan, your rummy brother killed off my Cutty last week, but we got some Grandad, Stoli. . . " He pulled up to the sideboard and surveyed the options. ". . . little bit of Gilbey's—it's, uh, gin. Um, this scotch here is not the best. . . "

"Grandad with some water and ice is fine."

The Colonel snuffed his cigar in an ashtray by the ice bucket. Fixing the drink, he asked, "How about you, Franklin?"

"I think I'll make myself an Old Fashioned." Frank stepped forward.

"Hmph." The Colonel grunted his disapproval. "Well, you'll have to root around in the kitchen for the bitters and whatever other shit you need for your sissy drink, madam."

Frank went to the kitchen while the Colonel handed Jonathan his drink and began to fix his own. When Frank returned, he completed his concoction at the sideboard, then stepped away with his glass to his lips, sipping with pleasure. "Mmmm. . . happy days."

Having stood to the side observing the proceedings, Ruth now jumped forward and blurted, "I want a martini!"

Colonel Haygood, taking a slug from his glass, waved a dismissive hand, saying, "Go ahead." He parked himself between two chairs at the table as Frank and Jonathan chose their seats. Behind them, Ruth made a racket with the bottles and glasses.

"Jonathan here is a college professor. I haven't seen him for nearly fifty years," Frank began. "He finally got up the nerve to come and see his older brother before he croaks." He winked at Jonathan, sipped his drink again.

"Helluva long time, ain't it?" The Colonel's furry eyebrows shifted as he glared at the unshorn stranger. "Did you have a fight or somethin'?"

Jonathan shrugged. "Inertia, I guess."

"This is a good drink," Ruth said, approaching the table with a glass to her lips.

The Colonel redirected his glare at her, said, "I hope you used the cheap vodka. You drinkin' the expensive stuff is like moppin' the floor with Perrier."

"You don't have to be such a mean ogre, you know." Ruth pouted expressively, took another sip and sat down, silently frowning into her lap.

The Colonel stared at her for a moment, then said with unexpected gentleness, "Hey, go get us some pretzels, huh?" He nodded to the kitchen.

Ruth got up and wordlessly left the room, dragging her slippers on the floor. The sound of a large cellophane bag being ripped open and its contents emptied into a bowl echoed from the back of the house. Colonel Haygood turned to his guest and continued the questioning. "So why did you decide to look up your long-lost brother now? I hope you don't need money, 'cause he sure as hell doesn't have any." He started to chuckle. "You've already seen the crapshack he lives in."

"Well, no, it's not that," Jonathan replied, looking over the table at Frank, who smiled feebly.

Ruth returned with a large bowl of pretzels and a smaller bowl of mixed nuts. She placed them on the table and resumed her seat at the end, picking up her glass and taking another sip, head down.

"Well, it's a helluva thing," the Colonel was saying. "Being away from your family for a long time, seein' how things have changed. Like me—I came back from overseas fifteen years ago. My wife had run off; I find this one—" he jerked his head toward Ruth, "—tryin' to run the house alone. You never saw such a mess. And now for all my service, here I am—" smirking, he looked down at his lap, spread his arms, "—tryin' to hold things together on my pension alone, in this condition."

"Didn't the military compensate your injury?" Jonathan asked casually.

Frank let out a burst of laughter. "Why should they? War had nothing to do with it. The poor bastard went hunting with his buddies a month after he got back, safely retired. I guess they thought you was just a big, ugly doe, huh, Connie?"

The Colonel winced, took another drink. "You sacrifice your whole damn life for your country, and this is how they pay you back."

Frank explained to Jonathan, "The guy that shot him was an Air Force general," then turning, said, "That right, Conrad?"

"Hmph."

"That's a good reason for keepin' officers away from the front lines: they'd end up shootin' everyone except the enemy. What ever happened to him anyway?"

"He's dead," Colonel Haygood grunted with contemptuous finality. "That's the problem with you Frank: you have no respect for the military. But when the shit hits the fan, who you gonna depend on?"

Frank emptied his glass, got up to fix another drink. "Seconds anyone?" The Colonel held up his glass. "Gin and tonic, no ice."

"Fine. Anyone else? Say, when's Malcolm getting here? Are we going in for some poker tonight?"

"Naw. Between him and your college professor brother, I wouldn't stand a chance. I'm already half sloshed."

"Well, you shouldn't have started drinkin' before breakfast. Ha!" He shouted this last over his shoulder as he fixed the drinks, then turned around and affected a serious tone. "But you know, Conrad, you're right. I should be more respectful. And I do have a lot of respect for the uniform, and the people who wear it. I'd have done it myself, if they hadn't 4-F'ed me. 'Course we were fightin' the commies then—a proper enemy, not like the nutjobs we have today, goin' around blowin' themselves up and everyone around them." He returned to the table with filled glasses, set them down, sat back in his chair and took a sip from his glass, then looked at his brother. "What do you think, Jonathan? You're an educated east coast liberal." He smiled.

Jonathan considered the nearly empty glass in his hand, then spoke in a careful, deliberative voice that was heavy and deep, dampening all other noises in the room. "I think," he began, "that it's a mistaken sense of morality that leads people to sacrifice themselves for strangers. Patriotism, high-minded ideals like liberty, justice, honor. What makes these words worth dying for? If people were honest with themselves—truly honest—they'd have to admit that what they're really doing it all for is their own glory, to inflate their feelings of virtue, to force others to look up to them and salute them for their selfless devotion to some noble cause. And what are those others saying to themselves while they faun over their heroes? That they admire them? No, they're saying, 'those poor dumb bastards. I'm glad it's not me.'"

The Colonel reached into his shirt pocket and pulled out another cigar, put it in his mouth without lighting it, and wheeled himself to the sideboard to retrieve the ashtray. "So what is worth dying for, in your opinion?"

"If you're talking about war, why not ask your enemy what he thinks is worth killing for? The result of both motivations is the same: the soldier is dead." The Colonel wheeled back to the table with the ashtray in his lap, the cigar, still unlit, protruding from his mouth. Jonathan went on: "Now in Iraq, say, the insurgency thinks the goal of thwarting American corporate interests in that country is worth killing American soldiers for. The American soldiers presumably think that *promoting* American corporate interests there is worth dying for. So if you're an American soldier, you have the same result—you're dead—following from two completely opposite motivations: promoting or thwarting American corporate interests. So what would it be exactly that you're dying for? Their motives or yours? How would you know? I for one would not be willing to play the pawn in that chess game."

Colonel Haygood removed the cigar from his mouth. "So when Hitler was stampeding across Europe, you would have chosen to stay out of that fight because you couldn't be sure what you were fighting for?"

"That's different. I didn't say I was a pacifist. I said I don't believe in sacrificing myself for strangers. Europeans were not strangers. We had roots there. We had friends and relatives there. A multinational oil company, on the other hand, is a complete stranger to me." He looked straight at the Colonel and smiled, almost imperceptibly, beneath his wooly beard. "And I would point out that Hitler did a great deal of stampeding across Europe for quite some time before America intervened, so I'm not sure that our leaders then would have disagreed substantially with my view. Before you put your life on the line, be sure it's in your interest and not someone else's."

"Well, thank Christ everyone doesn't think like you do," the Colonel growled as he lit a match produced from his pocket. Leaning forward and bringing the flame close to the cigar end, he puffed smoke a few times, then waved the match, extinguishing it. He spoke with the lit cigar still in his teeth, squinting through the gray haze. "We'da been overrun by commies, Muslims, Chinese, what-have-you, if we followed your logic. You could wiggle your way out of any fight, thinking like you do—even a necessary one."

"I submit respectfully, Colonel, that since the second World War, none of our military engagements have been necessary for the interests of the average American fighting in them. Certainly not as a defense against foreign aggression. In every case we've invaded *them*, fought the war on their land.

Ours was never threatened."

"Then I guess you never heard of September 11, 2001."

"That's the exception that argues against ill-advised military aggression. As tragic as it was, those attacks were a fairly predictable response to decades of U.S. intervention in Muslim countries. Again, average Americans dying to pay for the meddling interests of strangers from faceless corporations. And America's response was to invade yet another country which had nothing to do with the attack. Not so bright."

"We got rid of a brutal dictator there. That's no small item. Now all we need is a workable exit strategy. You and I may agree on our desire to get out of there eventually, at least."

"Well, of course. As things stand, our presence in these places where we are not wanted only breeds more terrorists. We don't defeat them; we encourage them."

The Colonel was about to respond when they heard a knock at the front door. "There's Malcolm!" Ruth cried as she jumped up and ran to the front room. A minute later she passed through again carrying a gray overcoat to a back bedroom. Malcolm Peters appeared in the archway, stamping his feet to drive off the chill.

"Evening, gentlemen."

"Hey hey! There's the man of the hour!" The Colonel nearly spilled his drink on his lap in his excitement. "Haven't seen you since your boy won the election."

Malcolm smiled. "Yes, it's pretty exciting."

"You want excitement, wait till he and his socialist cronies start running things. Right, Frank?"

Frank remained seated at the table, slouching slightly in his chair, periodically lifting pretzels from the bowl to his mouth. He waved at the new guest. "'Lo, Malcolm." Then leaning forward to Jonathan, he said, by way of explanation, "Malcolm's probably the only person in the county who voted for Obama. You two should get along fine." He then introduced his brother to Malcolm, and they shook hands. Ruth returned to the room and took her seat again.

"Fix yourself a drink, Mal." The Colonel pointed to the sideboard with his burning cigar. "We was just discussing some politics."

"Oh God." Malcolm walked to the liquor selection.

Colonel Haygood harrumphed pointedly, then explained, "The professor here was just sermonizing on how to disencourage terrorists—"

"That's not a word, Connie." Without looking up, Frank popped another pretzel into his mouth.

The Colonel turned to Frank, annoyed. "Huh? What's not, 'terrorist'?"

"No, the other one."

"I think you meant 'discourage,'" Malcolm offered, diluting some bourbon in a tumbler.

The Colonel paused for a moment, considering. "Oh, well, yes, of course. What I was saying was we can at least agree on the need to get out of Iraq in a responsible manner—"

"Well, I don't think we should have gone in to begin with." As Jonathan said this, Malcolm nodded cautiously, approaching the table with his drink.

Frank spoke: "We had to go after the terrorists before they came here. That was the lesson of nine-eleven."

"I think the lesson of nine-eleven was that we had a leadership that was asleep at the switch." All eyes turned to Malcolm as he said this. He gave a modest shrug. "I mean, they had warnings, right?"

Frank leaned into Colonel Haygood and nudged him with a wink. "Notice how he asks leading questions. That's what teachers call the 'Socratic method.'"

The Colonel scowled. "I don't know what you call it. Sounds to me like blaming America for everything." He turned to Malcolm. "Look, Mal, you won't get any argument from me that we have dimwit leaders who've FUBARed things all to hell. But you can't put the responsibility for all terrorism on them. We were the ones who were attacked."

"Well, terrorism as a tactic is really nothing new. It's always been with us."

"So you just roll over and accept it?"

"No, although as I said that's basically what happened with nine-eleven: allowing it to happen through negligence, by people not doing their jobs. So you need to be vigilant; but you also need to try to understand why people are committing these acts, and then deal with the root causes."

Frank explained to Jonathan, who was following the discussion with quiet, observant interest, "Malcolm used to be in the Black Panthers. That right, Malcolm? They went around shootin' cops and terrorizin' white people. So now he wants us to 'understand' the terrorists."

Malcolm smiled painfully. "Sure, Frank. All organizations have their extreme factions, left and right. And sure, many of us were about meeting violence with violence back then. But I myself always believed that was the wrong way to go. My involvement in the Panthers was with education and community organizing, not toting a gun."

He leaned forward on the table now, forgetting his drink. "Look at all the people that have carried the label 'terrorist' throughout history. The British called the American colonials terrorists; we call them patriots. Do we call the activities of the Klan terrorism? The slaughter of American Indians by the U.S. government? What we've done in Iraq and Afghanistan? It all depends on your viewpoint. Every so-called terrorist can justify in his own mind his actions. Sometimes we might even agree with those justifications. But simply killing people we determine are terrorists is not going to stop terrorism, especially when those people are full-blown committed to dying for their cause. You just create martyrs and radicalize others to become terrorists themselves."

There was a moment of quiet. The Colonel put out his cigar in the ashtray, sat back in his chair, and brought his hand to his face. He rubbed his eyes, nose, jowls, and chin as if kneading clay. When he spoke his voice sounded reedy and distant.

"When I first went to Vietnam I was twenty years old. Before I left, my father asked me, 'What are you going over there for?' And I said, 'To protect the world from communism.' And he said, 'All right.' This was nineteen sixty-five, and a lot of people still hadn't even heard of Vietnam yet. But I did what they ordered me to do for the reasons that they told me. So when I got there, I met this grunt from Georgia who'd been there a few months, and he took me under his wing, so to speak, and showed me the ropes. And I remember he told me once, 'Y'know, the thing with these gooks is, no matter how many you kill, they just keep comin'.' And I said, 'Why is that?' And he said, 'Because when you kill a gook, you're not just killin' a gook. You're killin' a father, a son, a brother, a husband, a nephew, an uncle, someone's best friend, or neighbor, or schoolmate. You're killin' someone with history, with connections. You don't know how many people that gook may have touched in his life, and now you just wiped him out. But it's not like in a movie, where when you kill a guy you just write him out of the script. All these connections that gook had are still there. And these connections are actual people, and they get angry—and they want revenge. And that's why they keep comin' for you. And that's why violence always begets more violence.' Well, I didn't really agree with that, and I told him so, but he and I, we still became real close. But just before his tour was about to end, he got killed. I was with him. It was the first time I'd seen someone killed. And then my tour ended a few months later, and I went back to the States—got married and what-have-you—and when I got ready to go back for a second tour, my father asked me again, 'You got a wife now, and a baby on the way. What are you goin' back there for?' And this time I said, 'They killed my buddy over there. And I can't just let that go without a reply.' And when I said that—the *moment* those words came out of my mouth—I knew that this grunt from Georgia, this buddy of mine, was right in what he said after all, and it wasn't just true for the gooks, but for me as well."

There was a momentary silence; Malcolm nodded passively while Ruth continued to manipulate her fingers together in her lap and the others stared vacantly. The Colonel finished his drink, set the glass down with a mirthless grin. "Didn't expect to hear a speech like that from me, eh? Truth is few people hate war as much as career soldiers, or understand its ironies. But the saddest irony of all is that, in spite of all that, it's still necessary sometimes. Even though we hate it, it's still necessary."

"Maybe," Malcolm replied quietly, "that's why we need to think really hard before we resort to violence. We need to ask, what is its moral justification?"

Jonathan roused himself and reached for a handful of mixed nuts. "There is no morality in nature. That's a human construct."

Malcolm looked at him. "Does that make it less real? How do you live without moral guidance?"

"From where?"

"I don't know. Maybe from an honest examination of ourselves. With a serious commitment to compassion." Malcolm shrugged. "Maybe."

The Colonel grunted. "You eggheads need to get some God into your lives. He'll steer you right. Go read your Bible."

"I love God," Ruth ejaculated, then returned to her hands in her lap. Colonel Haygood looked at her with a frown.

"That's fine for some people," said Malcolm. "But even

religion can lead you astray, if you don't also have a healthy
dose of compassion."

Throughout the discourse, Frank had been leaning
forward with his elbows on the table, glassy-eyed, seemingly
lost in thought, with one hand holding his empty glass. It was
not apparent that he had been following the conversation until
he spoke up. "There are some things even God can't set right."
He looked at the Colonel. "If you do any injury, He's not gonna
just undo it by some miracle."

The Colonel raised his furry eyebrows. "Well, shit,
Frank, this is life we're talkin' about, not a goddamn magic
show." He shifted in his chair. "Anyway, I didn't mean to start
a whole religious discussion. The more sauced I get the less
careful I am about takin' the Good Lord's name in vain, and
that just makes me feel like more of a hypocrite. Let's talk about
somethin' else."

Smiling, Jonathan said, "Well, I'm sure we can find
other topics that aren't so problematic. Perhaps the philosophy
of clothes?" He rose from his seat, glass in hand. "Anyone for
another drink?"

"Here, allow me." The Colonel wheeled forward and
took the glass from his hand. "Another bourbon?"

As fresh drinks were poured—with the exception of
Ruth, who was lost in her own low-threshold inebriation—the
tenor of the conversation became acqaintive in nature, Malcolm
outlining for Jonathan's benefit his former career as a high
school educator in history, Jonathan in his turn discussing in
general terms life at the university level. After a while, the
conversation died down, tumblers were drained, and a silent
waitfulness ensued. Ruth had migrated to the armchair in the
corner of the room and sat with her head slumped forward.
Everyone else looked contemplative, listening for the first time
to the metronomic tick-tock of a clock in the next room.

At a little before eleven-thirty, Malcolm stood to excuse

himself. "Well, that's it for me. It was a pleasure spending time with you all, but I must be leaving. Thanks for the holiday cheer, Colonel."

With a wave of the hand, Colonel Haygood said, "Don't mention it. If you want to wake up the feed sack in the corner, she'll get your coat."

"No problem. I'll get it myself." He walked to the back of the house.

"We'll go too, Conrad," Frank said, rising to his feet with a groan. "Thanks a lot."

"Nice to meet you, Colonel." Jonathan offered a handshake as Frank retrieved their coats. "Thank Ruth for us as well."

"How long you stayin' on?" The Colonel looked up at Jonathan.

"I don't know. I still have some things I want to check up on."

"Hmm," he replied thoughtfully. "Well, don't get lost in the past too much. It can be hard to get back to the real world."

Ruth stirred in her chair, gazed up sleepily at Jonathan as Frank and Malcolm returned with the coats. She said in a groggy voice, "I remember you now. I saw you before yesterday. A couple weeks ago I saw you."

Frank chuckled. "That's impossible, Ruth. He left the town before you were even born." He turned to leave. "G'night all."

After the last of the guests could be heard closing the front door, Colonel Haygood shifted in his chair and fixed his eyes upon Ruth. He watched her as she sat motionless, apparently thinking of something. The audible ticking of the clock made the loneliness of the room stark and nearly pungent. He felt it weighing him down in his chair, pulling the sags in his flesh, the pouches under his eyes, with laconic tenaciousness.

It seemed a long time that they sat together, silent. Presently, he wheeled his chair from the table, said quietly, "Go to bed now."

CHAPTER SEVEN

As a history teacher in a Washington, D.C. public high school, Malcolm Louis Peters had maintained a tenuous balance between myopic optimism and managed frustration. Thirty-two years embroiled in the chaotic trench warfare of the classroom had many times tested his resolve. Yet he always remained focused on the task before him: that the children who faced him day after day, year after year, know their history. And not just *their* history—black history, some called it—for what was history if not the history of all peoples, regardless of race distinctions? Indeed, all histories of cultures, nations, and tribes, the vast panoply of the various human histories and their intertwined relations—this, all of it, was of contextual significance to History Teacher Peters. It was the history of humanity on this small planet, and he wanted his students to appreciate it in its entirety and know its relevance.

He realized his ambition was larger than his ability. His successes seemed rare. Yet he took exquisite delight in those successes and in the teacher's single greatest reward: the affirmation that something useful—knowledge and the love of learning—has been imparted upon young minds. And he was self-effacing enough to savor that joy which is the singular domain of only the best educators: the experience of being properly humbled before a student's superior intellectual gifts, to see the student excel where the teacher did not.

However, such glories seemed far too uncommon, and he knew the reasons had less to do with the capacities of his students and more to do with the influence of their surroundings, beset as they were with anti-intellectualism and mindless hedonism. When he finally retired and prepared his move out of the District with the goal of spending his waning years closer to his son's family in Youngstown, he could not escape a twinge of regret at not having achieved more in igniting the resistant young minds that had paraded before him like assembly-line appliances over the years. He sold his house—the one in Woodley Park within which he and Anna had raised their son, with the elm-shaded yard and embedded third-floor gables, and the purple iris beds on each side of the front steps, planted as bulbs by Anna when they first moved in. He engaged, with his son's aid, the services of a realtor in Ohio who found him a pleasant little one-story house with an acre of land and a chicken coop, and a moving company that took the proper care with Anna's heirloom furniture and antiques. He then loaded the remaining essentials, along with their dog Maggie, into his pickup truck and drove across the color-splashed Maryland hills to his new home one fine autumn day.

That was two years ago, and now Malcolm Louis Peters recalled it while sitting in the side booth sipping coffee and watching the gray November dawn through the window of the Sunnyland Diner. 'Malcolm,' he mused—the name of his father. 'Louis'—as in Armstrong, admired by his father, so he had said, for his musicality and showmanship, although Malcolm the younger suspected it was more for his ability to evoke the effusive love of white people, even as they imposed their segregating laws upon their object of adoration. His father had always played the apologist for white folk, why Malcolm did not know, but it diminished him greatly in his son's eyes. Countering his father, Malcolm Louis preferred to think of his middle namesake as Joe the 'Brown Bomber' Louis, the champ who knocked out the Aryan Schmeling in the first round and exemplified the image of the fighter who never quit. Malcolm

Louis Peters hadn't wanted to quit, but in the end, he felt that
he had when he retired. There were too many foes gathered
around him, penetrating his veneer. It was the adult prejudices about the children that often
left him most disturbed and depressed. There were the teachers
who themselves had been uninspired as children, remained
uninspired as adults, and therefore could never be expected to
provide any inspiration to their own students beyond the usual
punitive threats for non-effort. To these teachers, there was no
art in teaching; it was a purely mechanical endeavor. For the
students, years of exposure to such laxity usually led to the
conviction on their part that, no matter how minimal the effort
or inadequate its product, attempt alone should nonetheless
result in some substantive recompense. In the end, Mr. Peters
felt he had struggled in vain against this notion, flummoxed
by a world that too often failed to punish shoddiness and
incompetence, and sometimes even rewarded it.

Then there were those exhausting persons who retained
an undying, evangelical optimism in the ability of the human
spirit to surmount all obstacles. Often he would hear a principal
or fellow teacher recite from the catechism of the ardent faithful:
"Well, I haven't given up on *my* students"; "You need to believe
that *all* students can learn, Mr. Peters." "Of course all students
can learn," he'd reply, "but let's be real. If a child is having to
help his drug-addicted mother raise his siblings, has no quiet
place to study in the house, and comes to school every day
afraid he's gonna get jumped or worse, how the hell is that child
gonna focus on learning?" Mr. Peters resented the implication
from others that pointing out challenges to achievement and
asking when *they* would be addressed constituted a shirking of
responsibility on his part.

In later years, he found his task made all the more
difficult by the intrusion of technology's greatest distractions.
In its wisdom, modern society had made available to its youth

the limitless riches of cable television, satellite television,
video games, unsupervised internet access, cell phones, cell
phones with unsupervised internet access—indeed all manner
of electronic gadgetry to ease the boredom of existence. He
discovered that, because their cell phones had calculators,
the students no longer felt a need to develop math skills. And
because they had been trained to find all the information they
would ever require on the internet, and to believe it was all true,
they would no longer need to know how to use a library or even
read a book. And most heartbreaking to him, because he had
lived it, and seen it, was that so few of them seemed to feel the
call of History, that soulful appreciation of struggle and sacrifice
that had only recently eroded so many viciously entrenched
barriers to the far reaches of human endeavor. Did they not see
it? Did they not want to know? The uncompromised truth telling
of Frederick Douglass; the sublime, soaring intellect of DuBois;
the indignant, unblinking anger of Mother Jones and Richard
Wright; the fanatical righteousness of John Brown and James
Connelly; the unmoving resistance to oppressors displayed by
Geronimo and Touissant L'Overture; the forlorn doggedness
against all odds of Lincoln; the plain-speaking gift to rally the
masses demonstrated by Alinsky, Debs, Chavez and, indeed,
yes, today, Obama—these examples and others were a deep
and profound source of inspiration to Malcolm Louis Peters,
feeding his implacable desire to transmit that inspiration to all
his students. However, he always perceived his efforts for them
as inadequate, as no match for the grip that the lowest of human
motivators held on them. To many of his students, books and
great ideas were the realm of the unhip, the stodgy, the old. The
foundations of youthful dreams seemed no longer to be built on
hope for a better world, as he had remembered them, but rather
on a divestment of hope, on a creed of selfish gratification, and
humanity may just as well be damned.

He knew that, lurking behind the weight of such

glorified ignorance against which he found himself, like Sisyphus, struggling constantly, was the anarchic lure of the street, the thanototic and irascible riptide of feral nihilism and self-destruction. Growing up was about getting by, surviving the Now, denying the future because the future was unreal. He saw this abdication of responsibility in so many young people of late. Not like when he was a youth, joining the local Black Panther Party because their call to service, to critical examination of self and one's larger role in community carried the promise that a revolution was just around the corner, a revolution he considered all the more necessary after his years as a draftee in Vietnam. Today's young rebels hadn't even read Marx, had never asked the big questions. The mantra of today seemed to be fast money, fast glory, instilling fear, demanding respect without giving it, and every one out for himself. Every message from every medium only reinforced the mirage, and he saw many of his young students succumb to its lure.

There were exceptions, of course—he gladly acknowledged that. He was remembering now. He'd once assigned some readings from *The Miseducation of the Negro*, as he often did as part of his curriculum. One class actually advocated for—they practically begged him for it—a formal debate centered around the contrasting viewpoints of Carter G. Woodson and Booker T. Washington on empowering blacks in post-Reconstruction America. The result was an inspired success. He was smiling now, sitting in the diner, face to the window, watching but not seeing the crows flying against the slate-colored sky, remembering. He had spent many hours after school with that eager group, facilitating the metamorphosis of their thoughtful passion into exacting argument. The debate took place in the auditorium before an electrified student body. "Fine job, Mr. Peters," the principal had said afterwards. "Fine job."

Some of his students, of course, went on to college or

technical school, became professionals, firefighters, lawyers, teachers themselves, scientists, nurses—pillars of society—and some came back to visit him, to let him know how they were fairing, and to thank him. Many did not, and he wondered what happened to them. Some never made it out of high school. The smile relaxed. He recalled the chronically truant boy whose mother seemed unable to direct him to school, who pleaded helplessness when he spoke with her, she the matron of a stressed and disordered family upon which even school administrators and government service agencies had given up. This boy, whom Mr. Peters remembered seeing at the bus stop one afternoon, was polite and apologetic when Mr. Peters said he needed to start attending school again. "I know," he mumbled, head down. "I'll be there tomorrow." He wasn't; nor was he there on subsequent days. Then the news came that he'd been found dead in an alley one early winter morning, a bullet in his head. Students the next day exchanged knowing looks with one another. *So it went*, Mr. Peters thought. *So it goes.*

A crow landed on the sidewalk outside, picked at a piece of trash, flew off. Thinking, remembering, he was recalling too the girl who acted out, frequently disrupting his class, later revealed to have been raped by her mother's boyfriend. It was an explanation, yes, but the revelation provided little else. The school simply lacked the necessary staff of social workers to properly deal with every child's peculiar brand of dysfunction. And what of the numerous fights in the halls, in the classroom, fires set by the children, occasional display of weapons, threats of violence and actual violence to other students, teachers? He breathed deeply and sipped his coffee.

Approaching his thirtieth year of teaching, his wife could read the weariness on his face, and she gave voice to his inner conflict, finally urging him to take his retirement. 'You've given them enough years of your life. Let's have some to ourselves now.' 'Okay, yes, you're right. I'll do it.' What later turned out to be their last summer together was, at the time, lived with the quiet acceptance that this was to be his last as a teacher. But Anna's cancer was diagnosed as the school year began and rapidly advanced in an aggressive war of attrition on her body. She endured months of counter assaults waged valiantly by her medical generals throughout the winter, but a final resurgence quickly ended her life, just as the irises bloomed around the front steps.

Alone now in the big house, Mr. Peters decided to stay on at the school for another year, and then for the year after that, before finally handing in his retirement papers. During those last years he found getting up in the mornings to catch the Metro train and then the bus to school increasingly difficult. His calling as a crusader for the education of the next generation was becoming less urgent. He had lost many battles in his life, won a few, but was now growing tired. With the death of Anna, he felt like d'Albert at Agincourt, having begun with the promise of victory, yet finally beaten by contingencies beyond his control. In an attempt to steel his nerves each morning, he had taped an index card to the bathroom mirror to remind him of the question that used to keep him going in earlier days, that used to help refocus his mind when challenges faced him; really the most important question to ask in life. It was a quote from Lenin, the title of his great pamphlet, written at the beginning of the twentieth century, on the tasks ahead for the Revolution: "What Is To Be Done?" Every morning he faced that question as he stared at his weary face in the mirror. Well, he had to acknowledge that now he knew what was actually to be done, and that was to admit defeat and move on.

He was remembering in the diner booth now, when in his last years at their Woodley Park home, which he and Anna had kept season after season in the peaceful lane on the hill, he was finally able to pay off the mortgage, but too late for Anna to see it and celebrate with him. And he was remembering, in

that last year before his retirement, when he would spend the
evenings of winter in the garret room tucked away in the far
corner gable of the house, hidden from the street by the trunk
of the ancient elm tree, taking communion with the past. And
with the oil lamp burning—because she'd liked it that way, had
preferred the warm earthen glow to the dull incandescence
of the ceiling bulb, its low somber flame visible through the
yellow-tinted glass, holding back the dark—in this sanctuary
of memories he would drag the cardboard 'memento' box
from the closet floor and sift quietly among its contents: old
Polaroids washed orange with age, of easy smiling faces in
long-forgotten kitchens; more recent photos not yet savaged by
time; poetry she'd written; love notes; her drawings; a set of
pearl earrings—. And he knew that already his memory of her
was fading, that he was finding it harder to recollect the sound
of her soft, sonorous voice across the dining room, to imagine
her sincere caresses in the night, the sensate curves of her body,
the myriad innervations and impulses. Indeed, even her face
would all too rapidly dissolve in his mind if he neglected for
even a week to attend to his memento box. And after he had
replaced the items carefully and pushed the box back in its
corner on the closet floor, blown out the lamp with a puff of
breath, and felt his way slowly, resignedly, through the dark,
down the stairs to his bedroom—their bedroom—then pulled
back the quilt and the warm, whispering sheet, when he had
lain his head heavily on the pillow and wrapped his body in
the quilt's warm corpulence, sighing, looking out the window
at the ice-brittled branches moving in the wind above the halo
of the streetlight, he drifted into sleep and dreams, and happy
worriless memories, then to wake, too soon, upon another
indifferent dawn.

　　He was remembering this, still watching through the
window, having set his empty cup down on the table, when the
stout, ruddy woman in the yellow apron, her straw-like hair

tied up in a bun, approached holding a silver carafe. "More coffee, Malcolm?" She poured without waiting for an answer. "You're lookin' awful dreary this morning."

He turned and looked up at her. "Hmm? Oh, no, it's just—thank you, Cora—I'm just dreading another winter, I guess. They sure make 'em long and cold here." He sighed, forearms on the table, looking ahead.

She smiled. "Yeah, well, that makes us appreciate the spring more. You get used to it." She hugged the coffee carafe to warm herself, looking down at him. "You been to Youngstown lately?"

He leaned back and relaxed a little. "Oh yeah, drove up last month for a few days." He was smiling himself now. "I don't like to stay too long at one time—so I don't get in the way, you know. But they're all doing fine."

"And the little grandbaby?"

"Aw yeah, she's Kool and the Gang. Talks up a storm, never runs out of energy, but really nice disposition, you know. Doesn't cry a lot like some kids that age."

"Well, that's a blessing. Gretchen used to keep me—Arly and me—up all hours of the day and night."

"Hee hee. Yes, ain't that somethin'. Tommy did the same to Anna and me. Then later when they're grown you keep yourself up wondering where they are and what they're doing." His thoughts wandered again. "Gretchen still writing her poems?"

Cora straightened up slightly, shifting her weight back on her heels. "Sure, when she can fit in the time. She's been busy at school with the Thanksgiving pageant, then she'll be doin' the Christmas program with the children, but she hopes to catch up on her writing over the break next month. She wants to send some off in January to see if she can get 'em published."

"Well, tell her to come around sometime when she gets a minute. I see her nearly every morning walking past the house to school. I enjoy reading her work."

"Oh sure. She always appreciates your input." She surveyed the other tables as a prelude to leaving. "You want any more toast or sumpin'?"

"Naw, thanks, just the check, Cora. I better get going. I want to change the oil in my truck before the snow comes."

After paying the bill at the counter for his toast and coffee, returning to the side booth to carefully place the tip beside the sugar bowl, then grabbing his coat and hat and tucking them under one arm, Malcolm Peters passed hurriedly through the front entrance with a goodbye wave to Cora and stepped off the curb to his truck. Several emotionless stares from other customers followed him out of the diner. The air outside was heavy with cold moisture, threatening snow.

CHAPTER EIGHT

Maggie the black Lab waited, patiently seated by the back door, sniffing occasionally at the scratched molding around the jamb. When the door opened and her master walked in, distractedly wiping his hands on an oil-blackened rag, she took several steps back and looked up expectantly, tail wagging.

"In a minute, girl," Malcolm said, immediately closing the door behind him. "Got that done just in time; snow's about to come." He could feel it in the air. "We'll be able to get a short walk in though." He deposited the rag in the trash beside the door, went through the hall to the bathroom to clean up.

A moment later he returned with his coat still on, took the leash off the wall hook over the dog's water bowl, and went down on one knee to fasten it to her collar. He stood up and, pulling on his hat and gloves, opened the door to emerge from the house with the dog breathlessly leading the way. They walked through the chicken pen, past the three clucking hens that scattered at their approach. Malcolm glanced at the small doorway that opened into the coop, with the names of his chickens printed artfully in red paint on a wooden sign hanging above it: "Liberty-Civility-Empathy"—and the rooster, who always seemed out of sight: "Responsibility." Malcolm unhooked a gate at the far end near the wooded creek, led the dog through, and quickly closed it again. Maggie impatiently pulled the leash toward the footpath leading in the direction of the schools. Malcolm paused, listening to the familiar mellifluous gurgling of the creek in the gully below them, observed the sibilant sway of tall bare poplars and moisture-laden fir trees in the frosty breeze. Following the trail now, he watched Maggie dart about with her nose to the ground, delightedly taking in the variety of dense musky smells, squatting once to relieve herself and move on. A single mourning dove rose from the briars ahead of them with a furiously pitched flutter of wings, then flew off toward the barren field across the gully.

The woods widened before them, then opened into a small, treeless clearing. The footpath skirted the clearing's edge past a neatly arranged circle of logs and boulders which was a favorite gathering place for truant high-schoolers in warmer weather. Deserted now, its only signs of past human occupation were some mud-encrusted bottles and cans and a scattering of faded food wrappers. Malcolm pulled firmly at the dog's leash, disallowing her desire to linger, and directed her through a small grove of maples at the other side of the clearing.

The path finally brought them to the end of the woods, which opened upon the corner of an expansive, unmarked, nearly grassless athletic field, long out of use, with rusted iron goal posts at each end, and bordered on one side by a rusted and mangled chain-link fence. On the other side of the fence stood the newer field, with its bright yellow goal posts, a quarter-mile track and polished aluminum bleachers. Out here in the open, the wind seemed stronger to Malcolm, and colder, the sky more overcast and desolate. The first few flakes of snow were beginning to fall. He surveyed the vast panorama before him: the far-off trees encircling the field hundreds of yards away, the few houses hidden in silence behind them. As he stood there on the threshold between the woods and the field, he heard a rhythmic, metallic clang echoing in the bleak distance. It reminded him of the song about John Henry and his nine-pound hammer. He gazed in the direction of the noise and saw a remote figure below the sunken ceiling of clouds. It was a small woman in a heavy black coat pacing slowly around the far goal post, methodically hitting the iron with a large stick as she walked, her head down, apparently in deep concentration. Beyond her, the low-lying brick building of the high school was visible.

The tapping ceased. The woman had stopped pacing. She took what looked to be a small notebook out of her pocket and wrote something in it with a pencil. Now the field was silent save for the almost noiseless wind and the muted whine of the dog, anxious to be unfettered to explore this endless frontier. The woman looked up and noticed them, then waved. Acknowledged, Malcolm waved back, then knelt down and removed Maggie's leash, allowing her to trot off happily in the direction of the woman, stopping to smell several points of interest along the way.

Walking at a leisurely pace across the field, leash in hand, white puffs of exhaled vapor moistening his grizzled beard, and snowflakes flicking his eyelashes, Malcolm approached the young woman as she put the notebook and pencil back in her pocket and bent over the panting dog, rubbing her sides.

"I saw your aunt this morning," Malcolm remarked, smiling. "At the diner. She said you've been pretty busy with school."

The woman remained huddled over the dog, spoke more to her than to Malcolm.

"Yeah, the little devils have been running me ragged. I don't think they appreciate all the time and energy I spend on them. Sometimes I wonder what I'm busting my ass for." She stood up from the dog and faced Malcolm, smiling apologetically. Several long wisps of black hair dangled out from under her hat, blowing gently across the bridge of her thin nose and over her deep-set brown eyes. "I'm sorry. Here I am only in my second year, whining about it, and you put up with it for a million times longer."

"Not quite that much. But it does get a little easier in

some ways as the years go by. You become more self-assured, get a routine flowing—learn what works and what doesn't." He fingered his beard. "As far as appreciation from the students, well, I think it's better to look for your reward elsewhere. Kids aren't always as expressive about such things as we may like. They may not actually verbalize their appreciation, but it's still important what you're doing. Years from now they may recognize that."

"Yeah, I suppose. It's just tough when your whole sense of worth depends on so many other people's success. And not even other adult people, but snotty-nosed little brats. If they decide to get lazy and just screw off on the testing and fail, it's me—the lousy teacher—that people blame, not the fact that these kids are lazy and ill-mannered and had no sense of discipline instilled in them by their parents."

Malcolm chuckled lightly. "You're too young now to be cynical, Gretchen. You're doing fine, considering the limited control teachers have over the hand they're dealt. We're never gonna have the kind of satisfaction you get from seeing a finished product, like say a furniture maker gets. Or a songwriter. But we're working with humans here, and that's a product that never really gets finished."

Gretchen nodded thoughtfully, looked down.

"And take time," he continued, "to focus on what gives you pleasure. I told your aunt I'm interested in reading some more of your poems. You've been writing lately?"

She looked up at him and smiled. "Yeah, a little. That's what I was doing just now when you guys came up—counting out the beats, trying to get the meter right in my head."

"Now that's an endeavor where you do get the satisfaction of a finished product, right? An actual poem. And you're very good at it."

Maggie had run off to explore on her own the ground several dozen yards away. Gretchen gazed after her as she said absently, "No. . . I'm not really. But it is something I like to do."

Malcolm looked curiously at her. The sun had already begun to lower itself in the sky, saturating the dull shale-like clouds from above with weakly diffused light. The air was getting colder; the slightest tinge of rosy pink filtered down from the west through the sullen afternoon, settling as a glow upon Gretchen's face. Tiny snowflakes settled on her dark hair, melting to dewdrops in an instant.

"You know, Malcolm," she said, still looking to the distance, "when Aunt Cora got up this morning to go to work, it was very early, like it always is when she gets up. She thought I was asleep in my room, but I was lying in bed awake. During the week she says goodbye to me when she leaves—calls out to me through the door—because she knows I have to get up right after her. But on Saturdays she says she likes to let me sleep in, which is very kind of her."

She paused and swallowed, sniffled slightly. Malcolm assigned that to the cold. "It was still dark and quiet when she left this morning," she continued, then smiled slightly. "I was very snug under the covers." She looked up at Malcolm then and he saw that, in addition to her pinkened, runny nose, her normally intense eyes were soft and moistened. "I had my radio on very low, on the nightstand, and I was lying in bed listening. And they were playing. . . the most gorgeous music. It was a choir—just human voices. And it sounded like they were singing in a huge dark cathedral. . . all high and lonely sounding, and full of echoes. The music was 'Miserere mei, Deus,' by Allegri. Do you know it? 'Have mercy upon me, oh Lord' it means. It's really lovely, and yearning. Like reaching out for something that you know is unreachable. I just lay there, listening, and it made me cry." She giggled with slight embarrassment and looked at Malcolm again, smiling shyly. "It was just so beautiful."

Malcolm said nothing. A palpable tenderness of feeling crept over him and settled, with surprising firmness, in a place where he, a few short years ago, had abandoned all sentiment. Around them, the snow began falling a little more heavily, forming sparse patches of white on the frozen earth. Gretchen raised her hand and rubbed her nose on the back of her mitten and sniffed. "And that's what I'd like to do, you know? Create something that's just. . . beautiful. With all the ugliness in the world. Just to offer something that's beautiful. That's what I want."

Malcolm was thoughtful as they regarded each other silently. He said finally, "I understand what you're saying. And if that's how you're driven, then I'm sure you'll be able to do it. But remember that creativity can be more than making things. We can spread beauty through the world with our acts too. Take this Allegri. Now he made beautiful music, sure; and he became famous for it. But what about the people in his life who helped him out, gave him the support and nurturing that allowed him to make the beautiful music he did? I don't know if that would have been his family, teachers, neighbors, wife—whoever it was, there had to be some people who performed acts that helped him out, that allowed him to create his music. People history has forgotten. And who's to say those unknown acts didn't enhance the beauty in the world as much as his music? Such acts at least must push back some of the ugliness of the world, don't you think?"

Gretchen smiled at him knowingly. "You're getting back to my so-called cynicism about teaching, aren't you? So even struggling with the brats can be a form of creativity." She looked to the ground, to her snow-powdered boots. "Yeah, I see your point."

"I'm just saying there can be beauty in what people do, not just in what they make."

The snow now descended heavily as a silent cascade of

white. It was sticking to the ground, to the heads and shoulders of the two itinerants. "It's really starting to come down," Malcolm said, gathering the leash through his hands as Maggie returned from her explorations, her back frosted white. He reached down to clip the leash to her collar. "We better be heading back. Care to walk with us, Gretchen?"

"No, thanks. I'll hang out here a little longer. I want to enjoy the snow some. This is the best part, when it's just beginning to fall. Later it just gets heavy and oppressive, but now it's really nice."

"Okay. Well, carry on. Don't forget about me—I mean with your poetry." He turned to leave with the dog anxiously leading the way.

"I'll bring something around to you in a few days," she called to the retreating pair. "A poem I've been working on. It's almost finished." She cupped her hands to her mouth, shouted as Malcolm and Maggie reached the edge of the woods: "It's called 'Honest Faces.'"

Malcolm waved and walked on, then he and the dog plunged into the woods and hurriedly retraced their path back to the house. He moved briskly, watching his boots make patterned impressions on the snow-covered footpath, while Maggie trotted eagerly ahead of him. *'Honest Faces'?* he thought with a grin. *Curious title from the town's youngest cynic.*

CHAPTER NINE

He'd heard Frank rise early on Saturday morning, but the dull throb of a headache, probably attributable to the overpowerful drinks prepared by the Colonel the night before, kept him lingering in bed. Besides, he needed time alone to think, to consider certain developments of the previous day that left him stymied as to which course of action to pursue. He had to admit it now, he hadn't been properly prepared. Certainly not for the surprises that greeted him: the charred wreckage that was the house; the empty mausoleum that had once been the family business; indeed, he was unprepared for the whole decayed ruin that was this town of Vernen, Ohio. Added to these unsettling revelations were Frank's incessantly annoying questions ("Why the big hairy beard, Jonathan?"; "How'd you break your nose?"; "Do you have any pictures of your wife?"). They served to heighten his feeling of disorientation, along with Frank's pathetic, pleading apologies ("I'm sorry I can't offer more"; "I'm sorry I didn't respond to your letter". . .). What letter?

That last one bothered him a bit, so much so that he resolved there in bed to find a way to investigate it further. Almost as if in answer to his decision, he heard the front door open and close, followed by the sound of Frank getting into his car and starting the engine. When he heard the car pull away, he rose from bed and jogged to the front room to peek out the window. Yes, he was gone. He hurried back to the hallway and, without hesitating, opened the door to Frank's room. The dawn light through the curtain of the window was weak but sufficient to aid his survey of the room. An object on the bed instantly caught his eye.

It was an opened envelope addressed to Frank. He picked it up and looked at the postmark: "Jersey City, NJ." The envelope contained a single folded sheet of typewritten words in the form of a letter. He unfolded it and read:

October 28, 2008

Dear Frank-

I know you must be surprised to hear from your forgotten brother after so many years. I'll get right to the point. Having retired and entered what will probably be the final phase of my somewhat unspectacular life, I decided that now is the time to take stock of what is and isn't important in our trivial little existences. For me, what's important now is letting you know that I'm sorry for all the lost years between us, and that I don't want the past to control our future anymore. I know that what's happened with us is as much my fault as anybody's, and I hope you'll find a way to let me back into your life so we may enjoy what few years we have remaining as brothers should. That said, I'm asking if I could be allowed to visit you sometime soon. I am free from professional and family obligations to the extent that I can drive out from New Jersey at any time that suits you, weather permitting. Please send me a note back at the address below and let me know that I haven't let too much water pass under the bridge before gathering the courage to ask your forgiveness. I am truly looking forward to seeing you again.

Your only brother,
Jonathan

At the bottom of the page was typed an address in Jersey City.

He placed the letter back into the envelope, laid it thoughtfully on the bed. Staring now at the plastic beige touchtone telephone on the nightstand, his mind traveled back in time to that first call he had made to Frank the previous month.

He tried to imagine how it must have seemed from Frank's point of view, he shuffling hurriedly into his bedroom through the dark to answer the anonymous ringing with a tentative "Yes?"

"Frank? Frank Allerton?" The voice Frank would have identified as male, yet unfamiliar.

"Yes, that's me."

There would have been a pause at the other end. "This is your brother, Frank."

For a moment, he would feel he was outside of thinking, absent of thought, as one who trips and falls to the ground experiences the rush to impact, knowing what is happening, but not feeling, not having any feeling about it, simply waiting for what will happen next. Finally, the voice would come through the silence: "Frank, did you hear me?"

He would struggle to remember the name. "Jonathan? Is this Jonathan?" He might have looked down at the telephone, lit by the single faint nightlight. The surge of memory perhaps caught him unawares. Maybe he wished he had a chair handy to sit down and lean back in, but instead sat on the edge of the bed, leaning forward.

"Yes, Frank," the voice would have responded. "I hope you don't mind my calling. It's been a long time."

Frank's voice was weak. "Oh, sure." What does one say after so many years? "How have you been?"

"Just fine. Listen, I don't want to keep you, Frank, but I was wondering if I could come out to visit next month. Fly out to Pittsburgh. I recently retired from the college and—"

"Oh, oh, sure, Jonathan. Of course you can come. I'll pick you up in Pittsburgh. My goodness. So you're a professor now?"

"Well, retired. But we can catch up when I come out. I won't keep you on the phone. It'll probably be around mid-November. I'll call you when I get a flight."

"Oh, okay, Jonathan. I'm always here. But tell me what's new. Did you get married?"

"Yes, yes. I'll tell it all when I come out, okay, Frank? You take care of yourself and I'll be in touch in a couple weeks. Goodbye, Frank."

With that he had hung up. Frank probably sat there staring into darkness for quite a long time.

That was how it went—or so he'd assumed. He remembered it well. But the letter? Had it been in Frank's hand when they spoke? No, that wasn't possible. Look at when it's dated. Then what had he thought when he did receive it? Frank made no mention of it when they spoke by phone again last week, when he'd called to tell Frank the day and time of his arrival in Pittsburgh.

And now standing alone in Frank's room, he started wondering where Frank had gone. He hadn't announced his departure this morning, had said nothing about it last night. Would he be back soon? He stepped out into the hall and closed the bedroom door. He considered asking Frank about the letter when he got back, whenever that might be. For now, there seemed little to do but wait. He opened the front door and went out into the cold, heavy air to retrieve the newspaper from the porch. As he bent to pick it up, he glanced next door to the Haygoods' house and caught a glimpse of Ruth staring vacantly out of a side window. He waved but she seemed not to notice him, so he shrugged and quickly retreated into the warmth of the house, closing the door behind him.

CHAPTER TEN

He fell back on the bed, collapsed really, onto the soft red coverlet, fully dressed, the man white-bearded and fleshy-pale, expelling breath like an exhausted steam engine on its last cycle. It was Saturday night, and he had spent most of the evening roaming the dismal snow-blanketed town and countryside alone, Frank having relinquished his role as host without explanation. Left to himself, the visitor had wandered in his long woolen coat down white powdered footpaths and lifeless back roads, tramped across barren, seemingly sub-arctic fields until his boots and socks were sodden with ice and slush. At night he had explored the town center, feeling like a ghostly shade passing unperceived among the passersby single-mindedly pushing homeward against the enclosing death grip of darkness. He'd revisited many of the same dreary landmarks that Frank had shown him the previous afternoon, only now, under cover of night, these places seemed alive with some concealed, watchful presence. Long after dark he had stood in the parking lot behind the family hardware store, the one Frank had run for over thirty years only to end by watching helplessly as unrelenting forces harried it into bankruptcy and foreclosure. The store was unused now and silent. Looking through the frost-encrusted windows, he saw the dim forms of abandoned shelves and dust-carpeted floors, as patient and stoic as the furnishings of a tomb.

He had been standing that evening at the far end of the parking lot, in that horrible, lonely darkness, watching the rear of the store, which was shut up tight, with its small loading dock elevated three feet above the ground, and, reflected in the sheen of a small snow drift that hugged up against the dock, a point of light from a tiny, white bulb hanging over a locked steel door at the top of some concrete steps. The inertness of the bulb and its light, of the snow drift, even of the darkness itself, seemed to be scrutable and unchanging. Yet he knew that inherently all things were changing, indeed even influencing one another in their transformation. The crystals in the snow were in conversation with each other, with the light, with the frigid air. The snow drift blurred and diffused at its edges, but the light was piquant on the glazed surface. The diamond of brightness where the photons were most concentrated evoked the sorrow of loss, like a timeless sieve through which reality slipped into another universe, cold and pulsing.

He stood there, silent, a tiny mass of neuronal consciousness adrift in the cosmos. He felt reduced to the most fundamental aspects of his disparately linked particles. He had the sense that the self he called "I" was infinitely entangled with many other selves. He knew, staring at the snow with the single frozen light point reflected upon it, that he was observing the emotionless interplay among crystals and photons, electromagnetic waves and electron clouds, quarks of many colors, harmonic oscillations within molecules and chemical impulses among neurons. Yet that knowledge led him no closer to understanding the near-magical rapture with which it enshrouded his psyche. He was drawn down into the latticework of all that surrounded and beguiled him.

The store was no more. The childhood house was no more. And from where he stood in that grim parking lot, watching the tiny light above the steel door casting dire illumination upon the cold hardness of the concrete steps, he hovered suspended between corporeality and formlessness. *Jonathan is no more. Frank is no more.* All that he had known seemed to have vanished into nothingness.

'*This ignorant present. . .* ' It was little more than a murmur.

He looked around suddenly, noted his utter isolation, felt the numbness in his feet and hands. "I must go back to the house," he told himself.

The walk back up the side street off the main avenue, windingly ascending the hill in near-blackness under a starless sky, was made somewhere beneath his awareness. He reached Frank's front door, saw that the car was still gone and all lights were out. He felt absently in his pocket for the spare key that Frank had given him, unlocked the door, opened it. Thus he found himself entering the house, walking through the square front room past the claret-colored sofa and blank olive-toned television screen reflecting his small curved image back at him, and into the guest room where he sat down on the bed in darkness and fell back, collapsed with a sigh, onto the soft red coverlet.

After a while, the wintry silence of the house began to worry him with a rumbling unease. He wondered where Frank might be at this time of night. It didn't seem like him to be out so late.

He got up from the bed and walked from the room, crossed the hall and stood at the closed door of Frank's room. He reached for the doorknob, turned it, pushed open the door, quietly entered.

A nightlight in the corner gave the room a pious glow that called to mind a cathedral antechamber. He stood before the red-covered bed and looked down, seeing again the opened envelope he had examined earlier.

It seems that sometimes there is the possibility of several alternatives presenting themselves all at once. This at least was a fundamental of quantum mechanics, so he understood.

Experiment has shown that an electron may travel several paths simultaneously under certain conditions. Or was that just an artifact of the way we measure such things? In any case, he wondered if he might be doing the same. This thought occurred to him as he stood there in the semi-darkness staring down again at the envelope on the red-covered bed. It was the envelope addressed to Frank, containing a letter dated October 28—a letter that, strangely, he had not written. He knew this. How to explain it though?

He felt an uneasy presence cast a shadow upon him suddenly. Something was not right. Looking to the silent doorway of the bedroom and the murky glow of the hallway beyond, he was startled to see, was almost certain that he saw, a figure, a strange unearthly form engulfed in shadow. He squinted hard to see who it was, but could not make out the features. Then he heard a low, murmuring sob come from the figure, and it moved forward slightly, stepping out of darkness, revealing itself to be Ruth. Not the Ruth of his dreams, the Ruth he left behind in New Jersey, but the Ruth of the cat eye spectacles and drab housecoat, the one whom he had dismissed as a gentle simpleton, the one who had, curiously, told him just two nights ago that she remembered him.

The nightlight from the corner cast a warm mellow tint upon the apparition's face, which was contorted into a grotesque grimace of anguish. In the dim light he could see that she was staring straight at him from behind the spectacles with hollow, vacant eyes that were wet with tears. She said nothing, only stood there whimpering, transfixing him with those empty orbs. He felt an undefined terror. What mad lunacy was overtaking him? What sinister necromancy was playing tricks on his mind?

Then suddenly she was gone. The space which had held her became a void, turning within itself. The silence in the air changed to a solid, palpable weight pressing upon his body from all sides. Then the air crystallized and resolved, and as it did billions upon billions of fragmented shards exploded in a grand display before his eyes. He felt himself moved through the doorway, into the scintillating tangible dark, down the hallway toward the back of the house, to the darkened kitchen and up to the blackened window. And there, through the window, beyond the thick trees that ascended the slope behind the house, on a slightly higher knoll about a mile off in the obscure distance, he could see a ghostly luminescent pageant of festival lights, glimmering in the darkness. And it reminded him of his dream, a carnival on a hillside, peopled by faceless phantoms who watched him with cold detachment. He stood staring there for what seemed a very long time.

He finally felt overcome by a chilling rush of buried memories which jolted him out of his trancelike reverie. And suddenly there he was, standing alone in the soundless kitchen. He was wide awake now, and the distant knoll was dark. Nothing was there. *Was I sleepwalking?* he asked himself. He turned and looked around at the kitchen, and behind him to the dim hallway. No sign of weeping ghosts or bizarre light shows. The house was empty and silent again. He saw himself as an objective onlooker might see him—an old man, educated, experienced of the world, rational of thought—this distinguished-looking gentleman chasing specters around a strange house in the middle of the night. How uncharacteristic. How silly.

"Frank is somewhere out there," he said. "He's out there, doing God knows what." He was unsettled by his not knowing. But he had to find out. He walked slowly through the dark back to his room, where he undressed and climbed into the bed. He looked to the red numbers displayed on the clock-radio. It was 1:05 in the morning.

CHAPTER ELEVEN

Sunday morning arrived with a deep chill and a thin blanket of fresh snow under an ashen sky. Despite the weather, the white clapboard church was filled nearly to capacity, augmented by the appearance of several of its more irregular attendees.

"Why, Colonel Haygood and Ruth!" exclaimed Cora Roeder with genuine pleasure, standing with her niece at the foot of the handicap ramp as she watched Ruth gingerly guiding her father's wheelchair down onto the plowed gravel lot. "How nice to see you both. Such a challenging morning, weather-wise."

"Hello, Cora, Gretchen," the Colonel replied as Ruth navigated him to level ground. "Sometimes the spirit moves you, damn the snow and all, eh? That's why the Lord made front-wheel drive." Gretchen smiled politely as Cora pursed her lips and frowned. Colonel Haygood produced a cigar and lighter from inside his coat, commenced to smoke.

"I felt a need to come out today too," said Gretchen. "I don't know why. I haven't been to church in I don't know how long."

"When the Lord calls on you, you have to answer," Cora said with delighted pride. "Right, Colonel?"

"Yeah, I suppose." The Colonel waved blue smoke from his face with his cigar hand and said, "We had an interesting visitor to the house the other night, Cora. You may remember him, you been here so long. I sure as hell didn't know 'im." He took a puff. "Frank Allerton's brother from back East."

Cora looked surprised. "Joseph? No, Jonathan."

"Yeah, that's him. Strange old guy. Thinks he's some kind of intellectual."

"Well, jeez, I haven't seen him since we were in high school," Cora remarked with amazement.

Gretchen said, "I didn't know Frank had a brother."

"Oh, well, he left to go to college in New Jersey when we were kids and never came back," Cora explained. "He was always real smart. Frank and him fell out of sorts after their father died."

"Well, they seemed really friendly to each other when I saw 'em," the Colonel remarked. "And when Mal Peters showed up, it was love at first sight. Lefty One and Lefty Two. I thought Ché and Fidel had stopped in for drinks." He chuckled to himself, adding, "Or Obama and Biden."

"How's he look? I mean Jonathan. It must be—what, forty-some years?"

"Like your typical flabby college professor, I guess. Kinda paunchy, pale, overgrown whiskers."

From her position behind the Colonel's wheelchair, Ruth stared at the dispersing throng of worshipers and said to no one in particular, "I seen him before, a couple weeks ago. But I didn't talk to him."

"She keeps saying that," the Colonel explained with a disdainful nod at his daughter. "She's fixated."

"Where did you see him, Ruth?" Gretchen asked with interest.

Ruth took the spotlight and edified importantly, still speaking to the distance, "Oh, he was parked in his car on the street outside the house. Dad didn't see him, but I saw him though the window. He just sat in his car and looked at Frank's house for a few minutes. Then he drove away. He had sunglasses on because it was sunny, but I recognized his bushy white beard. Like Santa Claus." She giggled briefly then suddenly stopped and looked to the ground.

"Well, it couldn'ta been him," Colonel Haygood explained irritably. "He said he flew into Pittsburgh the day before we met 'im. Why would he have driven all the way out here two weeks before?"

Cora grew curious now. "I wonder if Frank saw him?"

"He didn't say so. In fact, he out and told Ruth it couldn'ta been him she seen when she brought the fool idea up. She's just delusional. Gets an idea in her head and takes it to a ridiculous extreme." He stopped, staring at Cora as if struck by a sudden thought. Then looking down to his lap, he said, "Probably just saw someone looked like him." He shoved his cigar in his mouth as a punctuation.

The four parishioners said their goodbyes and departed in their respective automobiles, the Colonel and Ruth catching a ride with a pious-looking elderly deacon and his wife. The early afternoon sun appeared to be darkening behind a thick layer of clouds, projecting a gloomy inclination of lingering on for the few remaining hours before dusk. During the slow, cumbersome crawl through the gravel parking lot to the exit, Gretchen said to Cora, "That's kind of weird about Frank's brother, isn't it? I mean what Ruth said."

Cora steered the car left onto the paved road toward their house less than a mile distant, along a twisting ascent of asphalt slick with slush. To their right stood a menacing orchard of apple trees, black and angular, with melting snow dripping from bare finger-like branches extending skyward into the gray mist.

She shifted her watchful gaze from the road ahead of her to the rearview mirror, keeping both hands on the steering wheel. "Mmm. Well, it's hard to know what to believe with Ruth. Like the Colonel said." But she was also thinking about what he had left unsaid. "Gets an idea into her head and takes it to a ridiculous extreme," he'd said. He might have added, "just like her mother," probably did think of adding it, then thought better in deference to Cora's feelings.

She remembered Ruth's mother as a woman of extremes: extreme anxiety during the long absences from home of her soldier husband; extreme anger at her perceived lot in life; extreme intolerance of everything foreign to her, including her daughter's unique brand of helpless dependency, which seemed always to get in the way of her extreme pursuit of hedonistic pleasure, a pursuit leading finally to her complete abandonment of family in order to partner with the town's other equally impulsive extremist, Cora's former husband.

Arly Roeder spent long weeks on the road as the district sales representative for a small office supply firm, traveling throughout most of Ohio, western Pennsylvania and northern Kentucky. His job took him to the towns and cities far removed from the insular, closely observed mores of the rural innocence within which he and Cora had come of age, fallen in love, and married many years ago. Despite their happy early years together, it seemed the appeal of far-off places tugged at his will with an unrelenting attraction. She recalled his increasingly distant demeanor as his position within the company expanded and his time away from home served to foster in him a growing discontent with his domestic ties. Her apprehensions about his fidelity simmered for a long time under a cloud of helpless doubt as she abided at home, alone, occupied by church socials and her work at the diner. With time, as she remained anxiously lamenting her childless and occasionally husbandless marriage, his reappearances turned into joyless reunions that soon terminated with ever more abrupt departures.

Her suspicions about Arly were finally realized when the announcement came to the house that a woman in Cincinnati was pregnant with what she claimed to be his child, and that she expected financial support from the father. The shock was

amplified when he confirmed that the child was indeed his, and
what's more, he intended to move south to help her raise the
child. Cora was left no choice but to agree to the divorce he
pushed for, but an added complication arose some years later
when word came that the mother was killed in a freak auto
accident which left the daughter miraculously unhurt. Cora
saw the opportunity to make a moral correction to an otherwise
iniquitous situation by insisting that custody of the child, whose
mother had no other family, be assumed by her and Arly, and
if Arly was unwilling, then by Cora herself.

The necessary and sometimes arduous legal measures
were put in place, and Cora became the guardian of what
she was to tell the inquisitive townsfolk was her niece, an
unfortunate orphan of a late sister from Cincinnati. Arly,
meanwhile, continued to follow his now revealed pattern of
dalliance by ending his period of mourning over his dead lover
with unseemly haste and returning to take up with the already
eager wife of the town's absent war hero, Mrs. Haygood. While
the Colonel was overseas helping to push the Iraqi army out of
Kuwait, she and Arly escaped back to Cincinnati under cover of
night, leaving the Haygoods' slow-minded twenty-three-year-
old daughter to manage the house alone. As word got out of the
situation at the Haygood residence, Ruth began receiving some
measure of help with the sympathetic intervention of an aghast
and incredulous community. Upon his return a month later, the
Colonel met his fate and newfound responsibilities with what
many viewed as stoic resilience, yet his bitterness remained a
defining ingredient of his character from then on.

Sitting now in the car with the mature young woman that
the ostensibly orphaned girl had become, whom she had raised
and nurtured through childhood and watched with amazement
as she developed into an upstanding college graduate and now
teacher, Cora felt touched by a diffused sadness. Gretchen
turned out to be as fine a daughter as any mother could wish

for, as outstanding a niece as any aunt could take pride in. Yet Cora knew that she was neither, was not even of her own flesh, though that secret would be theirs forever, if she had anything to say about it. And the common pain of betrayal that she and Colonel Haygood shared was also destined to be only theirs, though the whole town knew of that sordid tragedy, and only spoke of it among themselves, in hushed whispers, when neither of its pitiable protagonists was around.

Cora turned the car into the curving gravel driveway and was roused from her private reflections by Gretchen's announcement that she would be in her room all afternoon catching up on schoolwork. "I have a ton of book reports to read," she said. "I think if I can get them done in a few hours I can finish up this poem I've been working on. I promised Malcolm Peters I'd have it ready soon for him to read. But I'll be down in time to cook supper for us tonight, okay?"

Cora smiled sweetly as she turned the key to shut off the engine. "Sure, honey. You take your time with what you have to do. I'm glad you're making time for your poems. At least you'll get a break soon with the holidays."

"Yeah. That'll be good." She opened the car door to get out, then paused, turned to her aunt again. "And thanks for taking me to church today, Aunt Cora. It was a beautiful service."

She got out of the car and closed the door. Cora watched her as she mounted the steps to the porch and went inside the house. "Lord," she said softly under her breath, "please look after that child."

She leaned into the car door and pushed it open, then climbed out.

CHAPTER TWELVE

By early afternoon he could wait no longer. The sun shone blindingly upon the thin snow cover just outside his window, and the silence of the house lay upon him with a stifled, murmuring stillness. He got up from the bedroom chair and crossed the hall to Frank's room. His knock went unanswered, so he cautiously opened the door.

Despite the bright day outside, the room was dark and funereal, the shade at the window pulled down and the curtains drawn tightly to block out the cold light. He stood for a moment letting his eyes adjust to the dark, then approached the bed. He heard soft, even breathing coming from under the covers, and sat down on the edge of the mattress.

The breathing ceased suddenly with a snort, and Frank jerked himself up. "Oh Christ!"

"What's wrong, Frank?"

Frank squinted hard against the dark and leaned forward. "Jonathan, is that you?"

"Yes, Frank."

Frank wiped the palm of his hand over his face, let out a low moan.

"I feel like I'm going crazy, Jonathan."

"We're all a little crazy, Frank. It's what makes us human."

"Really? Do you really think that's true?"

"Frank, where the hell have you been? I didn't hear you when you came in last night, but it had to be well past two.

Where were you?"

Frank sat himself up in the bed and rubbed his eyes. "I. . . uh. . . had some appointments this weekend. I'm sorry, Jonathan. I know I've been a terrible host."

"But you've been gone all night. There can't be any place indoors that's open that late in this backwater. And you said you always go to bed early. Were you at someone's house?"

"No. . . no. I was just out in my car. Out in the woods."

"But it's freezing cold outside. What were you doing?"

Frank watched his hands as he kneaded his fingers in his lap. "Just. . . workin' on a plan."

"What do you mean?"

"Nothin'." He looked up. "Look, Jonathan, I'm really dead tired right now. I'm sorry I've abandoned you. But, tell you what. Let me sleep off the afternoon and I'll take you out there tonight. Okay? It's a place you may have been to before. I'd like to go there with you and—oh, I don't know—talk. Go ahead and help yourself to the refrigerator. There's plenty of food. And the car keys are hanging up by the front door if you want to go for a drive. But I've really got to sleep now."

He looked for a pleading moment at the other, then rolled over in the bed and lay down again. Jonathan sighed, got up, and quietly left the room, closing the door behind him.

"Tonight," he said to himself. "Tonight."

They were driving through the dark in Frank's car, under black vaulting tree branches hanging over the road like layered thatch, the radio tuned to the local country music station. The waning moon was rising in the eastern sky, casting a forbidding light upon the landscape as Frank turned the car off the main road and climbed an unpaved and uneven snowy trail up a lonely hill. They had traveled only a few miles from the house, but the winding, spiraling ascent made the journey seem far longer. The headlights swept past trees at every curve, highlighting each trunk near the edge of the trail for an instant, bringing it forward into sudden, momentary relief against the impenetrably dark forest beyond. It seemed as if something was out there, deep in the woods, in the spaces between the trees, watching them.

When Frank had finally emerged from his bedroom earlier that evening, he looked weary and unrefreshed. Yet he claimed he was ready for their planned outing. "Just let me get somethin' to eat," he said. Jonathan watched as Frank made them salami sandwiches in the kitchen, talking as he worked. He spoke in an atypically diffident way, almost as if there was someone else speaking through him. And his topics of conversation were of a strange, almost existential nature that seemed out of character for him. He made reference to things he'd read concerning moral obligation, selfless compassion for fellow man, and one's role in the cycle of life. He wondered if reincarnation was possible.

As they reached the summit, Jonathan could see through the trees that the hill was topped by a wide clearing comprising several acres, the center of which was occupied by a tall, abandoned wood-framed church in an obviously protracted state of disrepair. In the clear moonlight, the empty ramshackle building with its decrepit steeple stood at the very pinnacle of the hill, monolithically overseeing the snow-covered yard. Under the shadow of the church sat a barely visible wooden pew that had been removed from the nave years ago and set in the yard facing the front entrance. He noticed that there were fairly fresh tire tracks in the snow from the car. So this was the place Frank had been retreating to those late nights—an ancient backwoods house of worship that had been out of use for over a century, probably long forgotten even by the locals here, for it was placed on a remote, nearly inaccessible hilltop with only one narrow dirt road leading to it, and even that approach was itself well-hidden and seldom used.

Frank parked the car in the churchyard and got out. "I'm gonna go take a piss," he said, walking off in the direction of the woods. Jonathan exited the car and meandered in the opposite direction, toward what looked like an opening in a grove of evergreens at the edge of the clearing. He felt himself beckoned into the woods, thought he caught a glimpse of movement in the interior shadows. He entered the opening and found what appeared to be a narrow path leading downward in a spiral of concentric circles, partially obstructed by low-lying branches which forced him to hunch forward and reach his arms out before him to protect his face. In a moment he was surrounded by thick trees and started suddenly as he realized he had lost his sense of direction. The restricted path twisted around a deep gully, dipped abruptly, then seemed to turn back on itself. He began to worry that he might not find his way back. Stopping for a moment to survey his situation, he thought he heard low whispering voices coming from many directions at once. He decided he had better trace his way back up the path whence he came.

The trail led through a dense patch of woods upon which the slope began to increase sharply, causing Jonathan to nearly slip several times on the inches-thin layering of frozen snow. Fortunately, the tread on his boots was in good condition and there were plentiful low branches at grasping level with which to pull himself uphill. After what seemed a long time, he finally emerged from the woods and found himself not far from where he had begun, at the edge of the clearing in front of the church, with the abandoned pew facing away from him. At first he did not see Frank. He walked forward, and as he came within twenty yards of the pew, he could make out in the shadow a figure in an overcoat, perched upon the back of the pew, gazing up at the church, with knees drawn up and feet on the solid bench seat. A small radiant half-moon hung in the sky above and behind the steeple, pouring down a blue wash that deepened the shadows and gave the snow-blanketed ground a luminous glow.

He advanced slowly, his boots crunching the frozen snow in a steady rhythmic pulse that resonated sharply in the bitingly cold air. Frank gave no indication that he was alert to the presence behind him. His arm moved and Jonathan could see him bring a pint bottle to his lips. Now standing stationary a few paces behind the other, Jonathan spoke tentatively.

"Frank. . . "

Without turning, Frank addressed the heavens in a tenuous, remote voice: "So much time. So many years, centuries, eons. So many stars in the universe."

Jonathan regarded curiously the darkened back of the figure who spoke. He looked past and saw that, beyond and above Frank, around and above the silhouetted church steeple that loomed before them with the suspended half-moon slowly moving behind it, across the vast dome of night that engulfed the small hill, there was indeed a dazzling display of innumerable stars in the cloudless sky tonight. He searched his mind for an appropriate reply, unsure of Frank's meaning.

"Yes. It humbles one, doesn't it?"

Frank answered with silence, continuing to face the church and stare aloft. After a moment he said, "I once read that if you counted every second. . . one. . . two. . . three. . . like that, day and night, without stopping—and you pretend every second is one year—you'd have had to start counting from around the time of Moses till now to count off the age of the universe." Now he turned all the way around to face Jonathan, but his features were in shadow. His body swayed unsteadily. "You're the professor. Is that true?"

"I suppose so."

"And we—I mean people—we've been around for how long, accordin' to that. . . time scale?"

He thought about it. "Probably about a day, on your

time scale."

Frank turned back toward the church. "And each of our lives—yours, mine, everybody's—lasts for about a minute then." He took another drink from the bottle and again turned around to Jonathan, leaning to the side a bit. "Did you ever stop to wonder, Jonathan, about all the people that have ever been alive, since the first ones? How many billions of lives, each one different, each one an individual, each with his own thoughts and worries? And joys and fears and sorrows? And feelings of love?" He stopped, looked off to the side at the distant black woods and said quietly, "So much love."

Jonathan said nothing, wondering if Frank was fading off to sleep, if he was closing his eyes and drifting. Finally Frank let out an exhausted, despairing sigh. "We're so destructive, Jonathan." He waved his arm expansively, his hand still clutching the bottle. "All this will be completely gone before long." He took another drink from the bottle, then exhaled through his nose and shook his head. "Can't we just live without messin' up everything around us?"

He turned his face, hidden in shadow, to the other, who said, "I don't know, Frank. I don't know the answer to your question. Come on, let's go. It's cold out here. I'll drive you home."

He reached out an arm to Frank and gently lifted him down from the pew. "I thought you'd left me," Frank was saying, placing his feet shakily on the ground.

"No, Frank," he replied, straining to steady Frank as they walked. "I got a little turned around, but I found my way back again."

They took a few more steps before Frank stopped. He raised the bottle to his lips, then paused and turned to his companion. "You know, I wanted to bring you out here because this is where I go when I'm confused, Jonathan. And for the past couple of days, I've been confused by you. I didn't know why you're here."

"You know why I'm here, Frank. Put the booze away."

Frank put the bottle back in his pocket and they resumed their precarious walk, each hanging onto the other. "I'm not an alcoholic, Jonathan," Frank said. "I just drink a lot."

He stopped again for a moment, looking around to gauge his bearings, swaying slightly. Then he continued unsteadily toward the car, supported by Jonathan's arm, speaking as he went.

"Some people come out here, you know, to marvel at the beauty of God's work. To worship His—" He stumbled slightly, "—His majesty and all. But. . . you know. . . there is no God." He stopped and stared straight up at Jonathan, who smelled the alcoholic breath but could barely discern the face of the one who spoke. "If there was a God," Frank said, "how could He not hate us?"

The derelict church and waning moon stood silent watch over the two men as they made their way through the darkness to the car and got in. From the driver's seat, Jonathan said, "Let me have your key, Frank." Frank reached in his pocket and handed it to him.

As he turned the key in the ignition and engaged the clutch, he heard Frank say, "I changed my will today. . . "

He stopped short, left the engine idling. "Your will? What will?"

"I haven't been completely honest with you. But now I am. I think I know now." He turned to face the man in the driver's seat. "You deserve better after all I've done to you. I could see the suffering in your eyes. When I told you the other day I had no money. You looked so. . . " He searched for the word. ". . . distraught. So now you'll get everything. It's quite a lot. But you deserve it."

"What are you talking about, Frank?"

Frank had turned facing forward again. He laid his head

back against the seat and closed his eyes. "You'll get it soon. I don't have much longer. . . "

No further words were exchanged between them on the drive back. Frank had fallen asleep. When they arrived back at the house, Jonathan roused him sufficiently to help him into his bedroom and out of his shoes, laid him prone upon the bed and covered him with a blanket. Then he closed the door and crossed the hall to his own room, wondering, seeing the paths before him diminish, vanishing one by one, and leaving a single, narrow remaining course with no exit.

CHAPTER THIRTEEN

"Take your place with the rest of them."

"But Ruth never called me back."

"What's that got to do with me? Get in the boat. She's in there."

"I'm right here, Jonathan."

"No, not you. The other Ruth. My wife."

"She's not your wife. If that's what she told you, it's a lie."

"I think I deserve better than this."

"That's your problem, Jake. You think the world owes you. But it doesn't, so stop trying to steal what isn't yours."

"That's rich, Johnny boy. You calling me a thief. You know, we're like two peas in a pod, you and me."

He woke with a start. The half-moon shone with an ominous distant light through the bedroom window. He stared, feeling watched by it, lying in bed surrounded by the pre-dawn hush, sensing but not hearing a menacing susurrus permeating the room and creeping into his skin. The sinister foreboding of the dream lingered with him. He had been in that place again, had seen the setting, the lake shore, the lights on the hillside, the candle-rimmed boats—only this time he was on the lake itself, not in a boat, but apparently viewing it from above, seeing the characters engaged in a performance of which he was not a part. Who were these people? There was someone, it seemed, like Ruth, though which one he couldn't tell. Others also, like Jake and Jonathan, or weird amalgamations of those people. Someone he didn't know, an omniscient father-figure hidden in the shadows. How many were there? He could not discern it now. But he knew that he was not a part of the dream this time, only an observer. And around a central rowboat, the focus of the play, floating in the calm black waters, he saw other similar boats, some empty, some occupied, but all bathed by the holy red glimmer of flickering candlelight. In the water itself, anonymous naked bodies were swimming about, submerging and reappearing, playfully splashing one another, embracing in sexual union then parting, hanging off the sides of boats then disappearing again. He thought he saw Ruth, his Ruth, the young, laughing Ruth, or someone like her, standing naked in a nearby boat, then diving into the water with the grace of a petrel, but she never resurfaced.

How simple it all would be without entanglement, without the messy human emotional attachments that plagued the calm synchronicity of living: pleasure that was absent sacrifice; the merited payoff without the expense of humiliating genuflection; sexual reward without the additional stifling sentiment. He felt weighed down with oppressive obligation. Another day, another hour in this overbearingly inert wasteland would be too much for him. It had been a mistake to come here. Far too much time had passed, and Frank was right about one thing: the stars in the universe around us and the eons behind us are beyond the feeble philosophies of the mere human mind. Time advances and the cosmos continue to expand beyond all limits, and we are left here with ourselves drowning in the wake of all progression. No matter what time it is, it's always too late. He had to leave. But he needed to see Frank one last time.

He rose from the bed and stepped softly across the quiescent room to the door. Earlier that evening Frank had begun to talk strangely about his feelings of déjà vu, about his sensation that this entire last week had been something he had seen before, or experienced on some undefined level, maybe as a dream, or even through the guise of another person. Listening to Frank ramble on like this, he noted how his own sense of identity had dissipated of late. But he had dismissed Frank's meanderings. "You know, it's probably just an anomaly in the brain chemistry," he'd said. "They're finding that now with epileptics. Déjà vu is just mind-constructed scenarios that never happened, but the patients are convinced that they did, and it's all linked to a misfiring of neurons, or something like that. We probably all have that occasionally, when we think the reality around us is altered." He'd smiled condescendingly. "But it just comes down to simple chemistry, Frank."

Opening the guest room door, he saw that the hallway was dark, but that a faint glow from the nightlight in Frank's room illuminated the gap beneath the closed door facing him. "No, no, Jonathan," Frank had protested. "I can't accept your cold, logical explanations for everything." He reached for the doorknob. He hadn't checked the time, but knew that it must be sometime in the small hours well past midnight. They had both returned from the journey to the church on the hill spent and fatigued, each lost in his own disheartened malaise, which in Frank's case was helped along by his frequent sips at the secreted pint bottle. "I know you can't accept it, Frank. Neither can I, but there it is."

With his hand on the doorknob, still unturned, he glanced to his right down the corridor to the kitchen at the back of the house. It seemed a much farther distance than he'd remembered. And through the curtainless window suspended like a vacant diorama above the countertop, across the hushed wintry void beyond, over the remote hills and valleys and bare trees and terrible silence, he sensed a perception of far-off carnival lights, and echoing, almost ghostly music.

CHAPTER FOURTEEN

Cora roused herself from bed very early Monday morning, as usual, with resigned reluctance. Well-habituated routine required that she first walk across the still room and stand at the bedroom window, this morning edged with frost, and stare for a moment in the direction of the arriving dawn, still dark and empty at this hour in this season. She contemplated the unmoving blackness, the few scattered streetlights from the downtown area, just visible through the eerie, silent, crystalline woods. Her eye roved across the twinkling treetops, down the gentle slope that defined the hill upon which her house sat.

She murmured a short prayer under her breath as she stared, punctuated it with an "Amen," then looked at her watch. Even in her flannel pajamas, it wasn't but a few minutes before she began to feel the cold. She reached behind her for the bathrobe hanging on the bedpost, stepped into her slippers, and shuffled through the dimly lit hall, past the closed door of Gretchen's room, and down the stairs to turn up the thermostat and make the coffee.

Minutes later, carrying a small wooden tray atop which sat a ceramic coffee mug, brimmed and steaming, and a dish of jellied rice cakes, she walked to the den and took her place in the chair beside the window. She clicked on the radio and sat back, passing her eyes over the framed photos that covered the paneled wall in front of her. The radio played at a low volume the saccharine strains of some vintage pop song. She stared through tiny, pouched eyes at the pictures and ate her breakfast

with calm deliberation. As she did so, she cast her mind back to
the church service of the previous morning.

The choice for the sermon text had intrigued her. It was
from the last chapter of The Revelation to John, in which he says
of the angel that appeared before him: "And he said to me, 'Do
not seal up the words of the prophecy of this book, for the time
is near. Let the evildoer still do evil, and the filthy still be filthy,
and the righteous still do right, and the holy still be holy." Let the
righteous and holy proceed as they are, of course, but how, she
wondered, do we resign ourselves to such passive acceptance
of sin? Allow the transgressions to continue, God seems to be
saying, for I will be the final arbiter of all wrongdoing. "Behold,
I am coming soon, bringing my recompense, to repay every one
for what he has done." But when? *There is evil right here before us,
right here in this town*, she thought. What of it? "Let the evildoer
still do evil"? Yet Jesus said, "If your brother sins, rebuke him."
What is it you want us to do, Lord?

We must abide in our own house, the minister had
stood at the front of the church and advised. Do not allow the
sinning of the world to distract us from our own road to Glory.
God will look after His own, the righteous as well as the sinful,
the consequences to be meted out each according to the acts of
the judged. To be overly concerned with the worldly affairs of
others is to overstep one's place in God's plan.

Thus had Cora left the service in conflicting states of
mind. Her eyes wandered across the paneled wall and the
photographs of herself and Gretchen at various stages over the
past twenty-odd years. She felt an ambivalent tug-of-war in
her heart when she considered the evil that had been visited
upon herself and Gretchen. And Gretchen's mother, and the
Colonel and Ruth. Players in the drama of varying degrees of
innocence, to be sure, but how innocent does one have to be to
deserve some sort of reparation for the evildoer's deeds? "Let
the evildoer still do evil"? With so much evil in the world, Cora

wondered if she could accept such a decree.

Yesterday Ruth had insisted that she had seen Frank's brother several weeks before. Ghosts from the past continually haunted the present. Had she noticed something the others had missed? Sometimes Cora wondered if Ruth was as dim as everyone seemed to assume.

Thirty minutes later she was dressed for work and knocked gently on Gretchen's door as she passed. "Sweetie, you up?" A muffled groan from inside the room announced that she was. "Have a nice day, Auntie," Gretchen called out drowsily. "You too, dear," Cora replied, then ambled down the hall to the stairs, pulled on her coat at the front door, and went out into the cold, clear, still-dark morning.

CHAPTER FIFTEEN

On Monday afternoon he got the call. He had just entered the house through the back door to the kitchen when the phone rang.

"You should come over to Frank's house right away, Mal." Colonel Haygood's voice sounded uncharacteristically shaken. "I'm afraid Frank's dead."

Malcolm found himself speaking words into the phone before the thought fully registered in his mind.

"Jesus. How—?"

"Ruth is in a state. She found him. The police are there. Can you come over now?"

When he arrived, there were two police cars parked in the driveway and an ambulance pulling away. Ruth came running out to the yard in her housecoat, her hands raised and twitching violently, her face twisted in an expression of frantic, confused horror, and the bright afternoon sun reflecting with a glint off the lenses of her glasses.

"Frank killed himself!" she blurted. "He's dead! Frank's dead!"

Malcolm grabbed Ruth firmly by the arms and tried to calm her. "Take it easy, Ruth." he said, then looked around. "Where—?"

Just then a police officer approached from the side of Frank's house with a questioning look. "Sir. . . ?"

"I'm a friend of Frank's," Malcolm quickly explained. "What happened?"

He had apparently hanged himself in his bedroom. The officer told Malcolm that it looked like Frank had tied one end of a rope to the outside doorknob of his bedroom door, then fashioned a noose at the other end and slung it over the door and around his neck, standing on a short footstool which was lying on its side below him. He was discovered strangled and dangling like a plucked chicken with his toes barely touching the floor.

"Miss, please get back to your house," another officer was saying to the hunched and sobbing Ruth as he led her with gentle care across the front lawn to the Colonel's house. Malcolm and the first policeman watched as he held the front door open for her and guided her inside, then returned to them solemnly shaking his head. "She's the one that found him," he said to Malcolm as he approached. "Saw him from outside the house, through the window. Imagine gettin' greeted by that first thing in the morning. Colonel can't get her to stay in her own house so we can finish here. She's really hysterical, poor thing."

Malcolm looked around as two other officers came out of Frank's house and locked the door behind them. "Where's Frank's brother?" he asked.

"That's what the Colonel said," came the reply. "Said he had a relation visiting him, but that he hadn't seen him since last Friday, so maybe he'd already left. There was no sign of him in the house."

"We'll have to track him down," added the other officer. "Tell him what happened. Real shame. Maybe he could've prevented this if he was here."

"Why would he do this?" Malcolm's voice was soft with incredulity. "Did he leave a note or anything?"

"Yeah, there was somethin' in there just saying he was sorry, or somethin' like that. I didn't see it. The evidence guys took all that with 'em."

Leaving the police officers to their duties, Malcolm

walked slowly to Colonel Haygood's house, absorbed in thought, his whiskered jaw set and white puffs of exhaled breath pulsing from his nostrils. Ruth answered his knock on the door with muted composure, though her eyes looked swollen and red. She moved aside to let Malcolm in without speaking or looking up at him. He found the Colonel in the dining room, slumped in his wheelchair with a full glass in hand, staring into space.

"Damnedest thing," he muttered, then raised his head as Malcolm entered the room. "Now why in hell would he *do* something like that? Frank of all people."

Malcolm shrugged and shook his head. He walked over to Colonel Haygood and put a hand on his shoulder. "I don't know, Colonel. I guess. . . " He paused, then gave up on an explanation. "I don't know." They were silent for a moment. The ticking of the clock echoed dispassionately in the other room.

Suddenly the Colonel spoke. "I wonder if it had anything to do with his brother visiting." He leaned forward to Malcolm. "Now I know *you* liked him, Mal, but I—"

"I never claimed to like him," Malcolm cut in. "I mean, he was an okay guy. I had nothing against him. He seemed to have some interesting views. . . "

The Colonel guffawed. "That's what I mean. 'Interesting views.'" He shifted in his seat. "Well, I didn't care for him. And now with this—" He glanced around helplessly, groping for the words. "It just seems like a weird goddamn coincidence, is all."

"And now he's apparently gone? Left?"

"That's what the police say. I didn't see him or Frank since they left last Friday night. I don't know what they been doin' or when he might have took off."

"Who's going to handle Frank's affairs?"

The Colonel swallowed what was left of his drink and

wheeled himself to the sideboard to fix another. "I guess that's left to me and his lawyer." He turned around and looked at Malcolm. "You know he made me executor to his will?"

Malcolm's face took on an expression of surprise. "Frank had a will? I didn't think he had much to leave, other than his house."

At that the Colonel let out a laugh. "That's what he wanted people to think." He spun his chair to face the other and lifted the refilled glass from the sideboard. "Frank had a small fortune stowed away in a savings account. You want a drink?"

"No thanks." Malcolm's curiosity was piqued. "Frank had money? He always claimed he didn't. *You* said that too."

"It was his best kept secret. And he swore me to it too. I was the only one who knew. We lied to everybody about it. His father left him a bunch of money, and then he did pretty well with the store while it lasted. Hardly ever spent any of it, living the monkish life he did. No kids, no women, no expensive cruises and such. Didn't even play the Lotto. The only vice he had was cheap liquor."

He took a solid gulp from his glass, stared at it. "Hmph. I didn't feel good about lying, but that's the way Frank wanted it. I never told a lie before, but hell, everybody does it, don't they?" He cast his eyes in the direction of Ruth's room, smirking. "Well, maybe not everybody. But then, she just doesn't know any better." He chuckled to himself.

"You think he left it all to his brother? Did he have any other family?"

"No. His brother was his only relation. But I don't know what the will specifies." He sighed heavily. "I guess we'll find all that out in the next few weeks."

Malcolm, still standing in the middle of the room in his overcoat, now running his hand over the closely cropped hair on top of his head, asked, "But if his brother left, how did he go? Did Frank drive him back to the airport in Pittsburgh?"

"I guess he could have. I didn't notice, but I know Frank's car was gone a lot at odd hours the last few days. For all I know, he could've caught a bus to somewhere from downtown."

Malcolm nodded, then looked around to the door behind him. "Ruth gonna be all right?"

"Aww, she's a mess right now. But she'll be fine. She was around the side of the house this morning and happened to look across the yard into Frank's window. Saw him hangin' there like a side of beef. Jesus creepin' Christ!" He took another swallow from his glass. "That would send anyone over a cliff."

"I'll go check on her real quick, then I'll leave. Unless you need anything. . . ?"

Colonel Haygood shook his head, staring straight in front of him. "Nah. I'm okay." Then he gazed up at him with his hard, blue eyes, tinged by a new aspect of oblique vulnerability. "Thanks, Mal. Sorry to bother you. I just thought you should know."

Ruth was in her bedroom watching television with the door open. The sound was turned down, but she was seated upright on the bed with her eyes fixed on the screen when Malcolm appeared at the door. She looked up at him and smiled.

"You okay, Ruth?" he asked. She nodded vaguely in reply.

He stroked his scalp with his hand again and queried, "You. . . uh. . . you didn't see when Frank's brother left, did you?"

Ruth shook her head and gazed up at him. "I seen him come in late one night a few days ago—walkin'. A couple weeks ago he had his car. I don't know where his car is. Maybe he parked it somewhere, and then drove it back." Her inflection took a mournful lilt at this last phrase.

"No, he flew out here from New Jersey. He didn't drive."

She stared vacantly at the television screen. "He was drivin' a green car. A couple weeks ago."

His mind was puzzled as he watched her. She had said something Friday night about remembering him. What had she meant? Had it been just the alcohol confusing her memory?

"Did he go into Frank's house when you saw him with his car?" he asked.

"No, he just parked in the road for a few minutes, then drove away." She laughed to herself. "He looked like Santa Claus, with sunglasses."

Malcolm considered this, then said, "Maybe it was someone else."

She shook her head, calmly but firmly, still watching the silent television. "No, it was him."

Malcolm stood for a moment longer, lost in thought. Then he inhaled and said, "Well, I'm gonna go now, Ruth. You take care of yourself."

He gently reached out to touch her on the arm, but she was unresponsive. It felt to him like she wasn't really there.

Buttoning his coat, he strolled through the house to the front door, pausing to say goodbye to Colonel Haygood, who was still sitting in the dining room, staring at nothing. The Colonel waved wordlessly. Malcolm stepped out onto the porch, into the frosty, sun-drenched afternoon, and closed the door behind him.

CHAPTER SIXTEEN

About a week later, Malcolm was sitting in his first-floor bedroom, in a chair by the closet, perusing Anna's memento box, when he heard Maggie bark once, followed by the ringing of the doorbell. He looked at his watch, saw that it was nearing five-thirty, then glanced out the window to see that a grim dusk had settled upon the snowless, frozen yard. He placed the box on the bed and went to answer the door.

Gretchen, standing in her long overcoat, black scarf and black woolen hat, smiled up at him. "Come in, Gretchen," he said softly.

He shooed the dog back as he stepped aside for her to enter. She removed her hat and pulled her backpack off her shoulders, saying, "Aunt Cora and I wanted to ask if you'd like to come over for Thanksgiving dinner on Thursday."

He gazed down at her seriously. "Well, that's very nice. Thank you." Closing the door behind her, he continued, "I think we're all a little disjointed after what happened the other day. Some company would be a good thing."

"What happened anyway? Did Frank really. . . ?" She looked noticeably unnerved.

Malcolm sighed. "Apparently he took his own life. Colonel Haygood called me Monday afternoon, and I got over there as the police and ambulance were leaving."

"Why would he do that?" she asked. "It doesn't seem possible."

"I don't know. I sure didn't see it coming." He reached

down and rubbed Maggie behind the ears. The light in the room was muted; a single green-shaded lamp, rather than illuminating, seemed merely to embellish the darkness all around. "You think you understand what motivates some people, then they surprise you with some performance that's completely off the hook like that." He looked at the dog as he spoke. "I doubt that even Frank himself could tell you why." He straightened up and sighed loudly. "Anyway, funeral's tomorrow."

Gretchen's eyes roamed the room, took in the framed photographs in shadow on the wall: Malcolm's son Tommy with his wife and infant daughter; Malcolm with Tommy years ago as a little boy at the Lincoln Memorial in Washington, D.C.; Malcolm and Anna not so long ago in a garden, holding hands and smiling at the camera.

"I've never had anyone I know die before," she said. "I guess I didn't really know Frank that well, but I liked him."

Malcolm regarded her for a moment, then said, "Come on back here, if you have a minute. I'd like to show you something."

"Okay, just for a minute," she replied, keeping her coat on and picking up the backpack from the floor. "Aunt Cora's expecting me back soon."

He led the way back into the bedroom, where Gretchen immediately noticed the open cardboard box on the bed. "One of my rituals," he said, sitting on the bed and taking up the box, "is going through some memories I have of my wife Anna. Have a seat."

They sat next to each other on the bed and Gretchen eyed the box curiously. He explained that the box contained all the small items that once belonged to his wife which he allowed himself to retain after her death. "Most of these you wouldn't be interested in," he said, sorting through the mementoes with care—the assorted papers, photographs, drawings. He removed a photo and held it out to her.

"That's Anna," he said.

Gretchen examined it closely, then handed it back to him. "She's lovely," she said.

"Yeah."

He sifted through more items, then took out the pair of pearl earrings. "Now these are very nice. I got them for her on our tenth anniversary." Holding them out to Gretchen, he asked, "Do you like jewelry? Would you like these?"

Gretchen took them in her hand and gazed down at them, open-mouthed. "Wow, they're beautiful." The light from the ceiling globe played off the lustrous pearls and produced a pastel rainbow sheen on the surface. "You're giving these to me?"

"Sure, if you want them."

"Thank you, Malcolm." She looked at him and smiled. "I know you loved her a lot."

Malcolm focused his attention back on the contents of the box, shuffling through them. "The thing you miss most," he said, "at least in my case, is the intimacy. Having someone you can completely open up with, be completely naked with." He stopped, surprised at his own words, and flashed his eyes briefly in her direction, fearing that he had shocked her. Her indulgent smile suggested he had not. He went on quickly, "I don't mean physically, although that is a part of it. I mean in the sense that you don't have to put up any fronts. Anna and I knew each other inside and out. We didn't need to try to impress each other, or play games. We didn't feel like we had to do each other favors, to do things for each other. I mean we did all the time, but it wasn't out of a sense that we were racking up points or being better people because of it, or felt obligated. It was just what we did naturally. Even when she was dying we talked freely about how we both felt. And we expressed our needs, our fears, our joys openly. We. . . we were intimate up to the end."

"No pretensions," Gretchen ventured, watching him closely.

"None." Malcolm closed the box without looking up.

Gretchen felt a sudden desire to move closer to him, but it seemed indecorous. Talk of intimacy, physical and otherwise, reminded her of the extent to which it was lacking in her own life. Aunt Cora was a solid emotional anchor for Gretchen, to be sure, but her spirit had been crippled in its own way many years ago, and Gretchen had long since ceased looking to her aunt for the sort of deeper affection that true mutual understanding advances. Yet Gretchen had no other that she was close to. Physical intimacy at her age held a special dominion in her mind, but she had had little experience with it.

"You two must have had a wonderful life," was all she could think to say, as Malcolm rose to put the memento box back into the closet. He walked back to the bed and, standing, put his hands in his pockets, looking down at her.

"You and I have a special bond, Gretchen. You know that? I mean because we're teachers. That's an important responsibility. Like parenting, but not exactly like it. Anybody can become a parent. It doesn't take much to make a child and raise it. Any dumb animal can do it, and do it well even. Birds are good parents. Dogs are good parents. Pigs are good parents. They make babies and feed them and provide for their needs and help them grow up into strong, independent adults. But a teacher is charged with taking a child and turning it into an educated, reflective member of society. That's real heavy when you think about it. It's one thing that makes us different from other animals. We. . . impart upon our young a sense of obligation, responsibility, and. . . a respect for history." He looked up over the bed and through the window to the yard. "And sure, there's lots of parents that are also good teachers to their children. But if they aren't—and there's a hell of a lot that aren't—then it's up to the society's teachers to do that job."

He took his hands out of his pockets, folded his arms in front of him, and breathed in deeply. "What I'm saying, Gretchen, is that we need good teachers. Especially now, with all the dummies we got running things, we need the good teachers. And I think you're one of them." He looked down at her and stared hard into her brown eyes.

"Thanks, Malcolm," she replied. "That means something, coming from you."

"Well, I'm not saying I was any great teacher myself. I stuck with it, is all. And I had a lot of mess-ups." He paused thoughtfully, then quietly added, "Some kids you just can't seem to reach. And when you lose them, sometimes you lose them forever. I never was good at accepting that."

They both were silent for a moment, she seated on the bed, clutching the pearl earrings and staring expressionlessly at the open bedroom door, he standing over her, staring again with a distant gaze at the window opposite. Then Malcolm's mind moved forward to the present, and he said with a touch of desperation in his voice, "And what happened with Frank—how do you teach someone about that? How do you explain that kind of misery to someone? How do you make sense out of it?" He stood fixed to the floor in front of her, looking over her to the darkened window, thinking.

"And you know something else?" he said finally. "That brother of his—the one who was visiting when this all happened? He's gone. He just disappeared. He must have left before Frank died. The Colonel said he wasn't sure how long he'd be staying. But now no one knows how to get in touch with him." He paused, still staring and thinking, then shifted his stance and began to turn to leave. "I guess the police will have to try to reach him in New Jersey. I guess they can trace him somehow."

Malcolm turned to the door and said, "Well, I don't want to keep you. . . "

"Before I go, Malcolm," Gretchen called from the bed, causing him to pause and turn back to her. "I. . . um. . . I brought my poem." She reached into her backpack, dropped the earrings in a side pocket and took out a large yellow envelope, carefully, with quiet attentiveness, as a small child might extract an important homework assignment. "It's funny what you were saying before about intimacy. I feel like that's what was on my mind writing this. The many ways we can be intimate with one another, if we choose to be. And the tragedy when we don't. Anyway, I'd really feel gratified if you told me what you think." She held the envelope out to him. "It's meant to have a comical ring to it because that's the only way I know to approach tragedy—with a laugh, I mean." She giggled abashedly. "Kind of a weakness of mine, I guess."

Malcolm took the envelope and was about to open it when Gretchen suddenly stood up. "Oh you don't have to read it now," she said. "Just whenever you like. But I have to get back now and help Aunt Cora bake some pies for the church." She pulled the backpack straps over her slight shoulders, then took her hat out of her coat pocket and stepped forward to leave the bedroom. "But you will come for dinner Thursday, won't you?" she called back as she passed through the door. "Around three?" She walked out the door to the hall.

Malcolm left the envelope on the bed and hurried to follow Gretchen out. "Yes, that will be fine," he said. "What can I bring?"

"Oh, nothing." She was walking down the hall toward the front door, with Maggie keeping pace next to her. "Just some plastic containers so you can take some leftovers back for your doggie." She stopped at the door, pulled her hat over her head, and bent down to press her face to Maggie's. "Ain't that right, Maggie baby? Don't let him forget!" She opened the door as Malcolm came up behind her. "Bye, Malcolm!" She turned and went out, the screen door slamming behind her.

"Bye, Gretchen," he called through the screen. "See you Thursday. And tell your Aunt thanks!"

Malcolm closed the heavy front door as a last whoosh of cold air entered, then leaned forward and absently patted Maggie on the head. He thought for a moment, then returned to the bedroom. He eyed the brown envelope on the bed, but he decided to leave his reading of it until later. At the moment, his mind was occupied by other thoughts, either of helplessness or indifference, he knew not which.

CHAPTER SEVENTEEN

"It's time to go now, Ruth!"

As he shouted this over his shoulder toward the hallway behind him, Colonel Haygood snapped shut the hasps on his suitcase that lay on the bed. Malcolm stood nearby offering to help but was congenially waved off. "I envy you, Colonel," he said. "You and Ruth'll be basking in the sun and we'll all be freezing our butts off here." It was the first week of the new year, and the town was in the midst of a long, deep winter freeze.

"Well, if you live in a hellhole like this place it's good to have relations to the south when the winter hits." He grunted as he lifted the suitcase from the bed and set it on the floor. "I just wish we could've left earlier. My cousin says we can stay as long as we need to. This mess with Frank's will being held up—well, no telling how long that'll take to clear." He turned and bellowed to the door again, "Hey, Ruth! C'mon, let's go! Oswald'll be here soon." Turning back to Malcolm, he added, "Creepy kid from the church, but, hell, he offered to drive us to the Pittsburgh airport, so. . . " He shrugged and wheeled back from the bed.

"Y'know," he said, turning to face Malcolm, "it's real strange about this brother of Frank's. I mean him disappearing without a trace and then Frank dying. The police don't seem to be able to figure it out. They don't tell me much, but it appears that they contacted him back in New Jersey, and he claims that he wasn't out here that week. I find that very suspicious." He mused on that thought for a moment, then added, "I wonder if he said or did something that caused Frank to want to kill himself. Frank never was what I'd call a strong person, if you know what I mean. Always kind of morose, kind of fragile, despite his attempts to hide it. But suicide? I just don't get it."

Malcolm said nothing as the Colonel fished in his shirt pocket for a cigar, found one and clamped it in his teeth. "And another thing," he said, taking out a lighter and putting flame to the captive cigar. "Frank apparently changed his will right before he died. He'd had it divided up before between the rotary club and some other civic groups and what-not, and. . . uh," he paused to suck in smoke, "a little for me and Ruth. Nothing for his brother. But he changed it to cut out the civic stuff and left the bulk of his money to his brother. Now what do you think about that?" He looked up at Malcolm, but did not wait for a reply. "I'm not sure why he did it. Maybe something this guy said, or did. Maybe something Frank found out about him, or that he found out about Frank. Who knows? What happens to a man's mind when the past catches up with him and stares him in the face?"

"Was Frank particularly fretful when it came to his past?"

"No more than most, I guess. But you heard him that night you all were here. Talkin' about righting old wrongs, undoing old injuries. I think there was a lot in his past he was sorry about. But that doesn't justify his killin' himself, to my mind." He shifted in his chair. "Anyway, the court's holding up the will because there now seems to be a police investigation into his brother, as far as what he might have had to do with Frank's death."

Malcolm raised his eyebrows. "In what way?"

"I don't know. They just seem to think the whole situation's a tad suspicious. Until they get it cleared up, we won't get a dime. Not that I care much about it." He paused to look down at the smoldering cigar in his hand. "But it would help." Malcolm saw in his expression a touch of pained embarrassment, as is often seen in the faces of the proud when they are forced to rely on the good will of others. He wondered if the Colonel, whose well-known aspect of pride tempered by occasional slippages into self-pity frequently left others in the dark as to the real inner workings of his mind, was having money problems. He had noticed when he came in the house this time that the dark oak dining room set was gone, as was the sideboard, as was, in fact, much of the furniture that he had remembered from the last time he was here, the day they found Frank dead. And he suddenly felt ashamed of himself for not having considered this possibility before, the possibility that people who don't ask for help may sometimes be the ones who most need it. Ruth had been hospitalized briefly a couple of weeks after Frank's death—Cora had informed him of this, said it was a nervous reaction of some kind—but Malcolm had been unsure about inquiring too deeply, about appearing as the prying outsider, and so had never talked directly to the Colonel about it. In fact he hadn't talked to the Colonel at all after Frank's funeral until just a few days ago when the Colonel called and informed him of their impending departure. Maybe Ruth had needed some treatment that was unbearably costly. Maybe this cousin of the Colonel's in Florida was taking them in as an act of charity toward a troubled far-off relation who was too embarrassed to seek help from those who lived around him. Ensconced in his comfortable home and his semi-isolated wintry hibernation, Malcolm had been shut off from his surroundings. He now realized with regret that he had not asked after their well-being when it may have mattered.

"I tell you though," Colonel Haygood was continuing flatly, speaking to the floor as he wheeled the chair around, "if that guy had anything to do with Frank dying, I'd kill him myself if I could get my hands on him."

He maneuvered his chair to the door of the bedroom and

yelled into the hallway. "Ruth!" Turning to Malcolm, he offered his hand, and Malcolm was struck by the power of his grip. "Anyway, partner, enjoy your time in the icebox. And thanks for all your help." He released Malcolm's hand and declared, "Now I'm gonna go light a fire under her keister. We gotta get movin'."

"Do you need me to help out any?" Malcolm asked.

"No. That creepy fella'll be here in a minute and load us up. He likes to be helpful. You go ahead home. And thanks again for all your help. See you in a few months. I'll be a couple shades darker and you'll probably be a couple shades lighter. Hah! We'll almost be cousins."

Uncontrollable laughter at his own joke took hold of him, and Malcolm walked down the hall with the Colonel's chuckling merriment echoing behind him. "And stay out of trouble!" he yelled. Exiting the house, Malcolm heard one final outburst from the Colonel to his daughter, "Let's go, Ruth, on the double!"

PART II

CHAPTER EIGHTEEN

Winter had settled upon the land heavily, spreading itself with lugubrious intent across the frosted hills and low fields in a comfortable, unhurried recline, as if it had no intention of ever leaving again. The Christmas holidays had been colorfully staged upon the twinkling exteriors of houses and among the festooned and garlanded public places lining the downtown main street. Within the dwellings, tight-shut against the icy chill, lighthearted and joyful song or conversation had warmed the oaken interiors, and tables were bountifully spread with sumptuous, pungent feasts and free-flowing fountains of cheer.

But the season's celebrations were now a memory, and the subsequent dirge of January and February smothered the countryside with snowy oppression, crackling cold, and gloom. At night, people shut themselves inside and shivered in their blankets, imagining the lurking black stillness just beyond their windows, the myriad sorrowful lost spirits floating eyeless across the bleak snow drifts, and they turned desperately inward for warmth and solace.

Malcolm Peters felt the presence of spirits, although he knew intellectually it was just his own confined restlessness toying with his imagination. Imprisoning oneself in the home while the world outside lay dormant and frozen could touch off a nearly indiscernible activation of the mind's perceptual doorways leading into the fantastic. He felt the spirits moving among the furnishings of his house, disturbing the dog with a light brush on the hindquarters while she lay on the rug by the heat vent, or ever so slightly rustling some papers off the desk in the hallway while he sat in the living room reading by lamplight.

Many long evenings he occupied himself in the ocher dimness of the cellar below the creaking stairs, in a corner lit by a small desk lamp, enjoying the comfort of his neatly arranged workbench. It was a trusty, solid altar of heavy pine, its varnished surface now rubbed thin with years of use, impregnated with blotches of aromatic grease, solvents and oil stains, and scarred all over like the keel of an ancient schooner. He took pleasure in the feel of the manworn tools, the glint of the tempered steel socket sets all carefully ordered according to size, the heaviness of the cast iron pipe wrenches lovingly wrapped with oil cloth, the warm smoothness of the wooden handles of the hammers and saws. Everything had a place on the large pegboard above the bench, or in cubbyholes constructed in the bay just beneath, or in the numerous small drawers in the mahogany cabinet standing chest-high against the cinderblock wall. Extension cords and power tools hung neatly from hooks in the rafters overhead, out of the way but accessible at a moment's need. Some nights he would work for hours on a particular project without thought for time, focused on repairing a damaged piece of furniture or building a kite to take to his granddaughter in the spring. Other nights he simply sat at the workbench sorting out miscellaneous items such as screws or faucet stems in order to place them in their correct drawers. He found a well-organized work space to be among the happiest places for spending the quiet isolation of winter.

On a particularly cold snowbound night in late February, Malcolm glanced up from his sorting to the desktop computer perched like a silent idol on a small table nestled in the opposite corner of the room. He had transported it from D.C. two years before but had only recently set it up for internet access, mostly using it for email exchanges with his son or his sister in Richmond, and occasionally following specific news stories that interested him. But lately his mind had been casting back to the unsettling events of November, and the questions that still remained in his mind. Did Frank really kill himself? If so, why? And if not, then what really happened?

The death had been ruled a suicide. He had left a note in his typewriter, as the officer at the scene had informed Malcolm. The funeral was not attended by Frank's brother. No one in town knew him well enough to figure out how to contact him, or to want to be bothered with such a task. The police presumably had means to do so, and did, as Colonel Haygood had explained, but Malcolm was not privy to the details of the effort. Also, as related to him by the Colonel, the execution of Frank's will had run into a snag, although again the specifics were not widely circulated.

Looking to the computer, Malcolm had a sudden inspiration to see what he could find out about this Jonathan Allerton, the mysterious stranger who appeared in his home town after a nearly fifty-year absence, only to disappear abruptly just as his brother was about to commit suicide, and then later claim that he had never even been there. This was the man also whom Ruth had claimed to have seen surreptitiously lurking outside Frank's house weeks before. Even discounting Ruth's story as mistaken identity, it was still curious. Additionally curious was the fact that the visitor's short time as an acknowledged guest in Frank's house was not accompanied by much public fanfare within the small town. Hardly anyone had met him, although Malcolm did notice that winter's cloak of gloom tended to dissuade people's gregarious tendencies in these parts. Malcolm's memory of him from that Friday night last November, however, was becoming clouded with uncertainty and intangible doubt. Unanswered questions abounded, and Malcolm now felt compelled to unravel at least some of the dark mystery. He crossed the room and switched on the computer.

Some minutes of internet searching finally produced a link to a small article in a Newark newspaper from ten days ago that mentioned a Jonathan Allerton from Jersey City. Malcolm clicked on the link to access the full article, and when he did, a troubling new feeling of bewilderment began to overtake him. He read:

Former Professor Dies in Police Custody

Jonathan D. Allerton, 65, of Jersey City, died Monday while in police custody of an apparent heart attack. He was being detained for questioning in relation to the death of his elder brother, Frank Allerton of Vernen, Ohio, who died in November of what was ruled a suicide. A police spokesperson said Allerton, a retired chemistry professor, had been under investigation for some weeks regarding the suicide, which occurred while residents in Vernen alleged he was visiting his brother. However, police said Allerton denied having been in Ohio at the time.

Allerton's ex-wife, Ruth Ingram of Weehawken, told reporters that her former husband had been greatly distressed by his brother's death and the suspicions surrounding his alleged involvement in the matter. Police said Allerton had been taken into custody but had not been charged when he died suddenly Monday at police headquarters. An investigation into the death of Frank Allerton is ongoing.

Malcolm stared at the screen for a long time, wondering, confronted with a new reality that he knew must make sense, yet did not. Jonathan Allerton—dead? That much was apparently true, and that alone was enough to dislodge Malcolm from his center of balance. But the "Jonathan D. Allerton" of the article had also claimed not to have been in Ohio at the time of his brother's death. The article confirmed what the Colonel had told him before he left for Florida. Memories of those few days in late fall took on a haunting new reality for Malcolm, the meaning of which he was for the moment unable to discern.

A harvest of confusion rose up and settled on his mind. He leaned back in his chair and gazed up at the rafters. He turned his head and absorbed the lamplit workbench across the room with its tools all in proper order. Behind him the furnace relay clicked and the burner quietly, confidently roared into flame. Many things around him knew their place, performed their function with uncomplaining stolidity. What was it about humans that their very nature was deceitful and poisoned by malfeasance? The only answer he heard was silence.

He glanced at the large brown envelope that he had absently placed on the desk several days before. He reached out and picked it up. It contained a single sheet of paper with typewritten words—the poem Gretchen had left with him when she visited the week after Frank died. He had already read it through several times, given her encouraging critical remarks, said he hoped to see her work published someday. Removing the paper from the envelope, he read it again, distractedly, wondering at the mind of the writer behind the words:

Honest Faces
by Gretchen Roeder

The eye's a window granting view

to knowledge of the soul-(ah);
So say the wise, yet I, like you,
    prefer the areola.
Some will, no doubt, dub this puerile,
    but let us stick to cases.
We wish no ill, yet craft and guile—
    admit!—sport honest faces.

Herodotus wrote Histories
    To point us to our future;
But angst and woe, such mysteries,
    Are sealed 'neath seam and suture.
What Mary Shelley's monster knew
    would be something quite altered,
If hide and hair were sewn anew
    And in fresh vestments haltered.

No learned books, no philosoph,
    can in their texts bequeath us—
Those fires that burn in belch or boff,
    or genitals beneath us.
The touch of skin, the trembling nerve,
    speak tomes that ever sparkle.
Conveyed as such, inspire they verve,
    more than a chirping lark'll.

We seek in life a *passe partout*,
    a clarifying schema;
Yet, take a peek, it's, *entre nous*,
    mere whispers of a dream-(ah).
Perforce, what honest faces can't
    conceal through crack or hole-(ah)?
The eye, of course, can only grant
    small glimpses of the soul-(ah).

Smiling slightly, he noted as he had previously the rhyme and meter, the cheating monosyllabic add-ons punctuating some of the lines. Gretchen probably saw the latter as one of her droll touches. It reminded Malcolm of the breathy scat-singing of Sarah Vaughan, or the bizarre speech patterns peculiar to a brand of Southern Baptist preacher. He returned the poem to its envelope, sighing heavily, his mind slowly coming back to the matter at hand. Can a face even be honest? he wondered. What would that look like? What had he seen in Jonathan Allerton's face that might provide some intimation of the truth?

After a long while of sitting, he switched off the computer, then the desk lamp, and walked up the creaking stairs to prepare for bed. It was too much for him to consider now, although he knew that eventually he would have to forcibly confront the fact that things here were not as they appeared. But he couldn't do it now. At the top of the stairs the dog stood looking down at her master and wagging her tail, knowing that this was the time for her last excursion outside before bed. He led her through the kitchen, opened the back door and stepped out into the cold, still night air. Maggie ambled out from behind him and happily dashed about in the half-foot of snow, sometimes shoving her muzzle into the powder in search of some unseen, unknown, perhaps even imagined, quarry.

He turned his head upward and gazed. The sky was black as shadow upon shadow, with twinkling pinpoints of light scattered across its entire prospect like fairy dust. He stood alone on the steps hoping to catch a glimpse of a falling star, saw only the red taillight of an jet airplane miles above, moving very slowly. And there, beneath the vast infinity, the endless universe of unknowable reach and dimension, he stood alone and settled upon a small resolution in his mind.

CHAPTER NINETEEN

Time, the densely woven fabric upon which memory reclines and intercalates itself, sliding in and among the weaves like fungal hyphae—this time fabric makes no demands upon the travelers that move within it, save that there be acknowledgement, at some arbitrary endpoint, of some inconsequential thing having passed through, never to return. To acknowledge an occurrence having passed is enough, even if the passing through itself, while it was actually happening, proceeded unobserved.

So Cora lay in her bed on a bone-freezing February night, warmly cocooned under the quilts, listening to the wind blowing through the naked branches beyond her window, and remembered other cold days of the past: the low, very low periods of pleading despair, of standing on the frigid porch in her nightgown and slippers, too far gone to cry, staring down at the idling car, addressing the stony face looking out at her through the rolled down driver's seat window: "Please, Arly. Please." It's not fair, he'd said in reply. I need more. You can't love a man. You don't know how. I want more. She has passion. She gives me more. You never will. It's not fair. "Arly, no. Please. I love you, Arly." Goodbye. The car moved, the gravel crunched and was ground under the tires, the afternoon light faded to the color of pumice, crows squawked in the trees, filling the air with their echoes, and Cora stood staring, not shivering, but vacant and solitary. He said he'd send the necessary papers for the divorce. He was very civil, very businesslike and respectful.

She had to give him credit for that.

Years later she'd shown him what passion she possessed
when his young partner in sin died suddenly, and Cora fought
like a mother grizzly for custody of the young daughter, the
poor innocent who'd not wronged anyone, yet stood to suffer
a great deal were it not for Cora's inspired intervention. And
she'd sheltered that child, nurtured that child, loved that child
with all the passion a real mother might summon.

And so the fabric of time spread itself across the many
days and years, and now as she lay in bed her memory pushed
backward to recall the growth of this child and her development
into womanhood. It all seemed to have happened so fast. She
was received as a shy, inquisitive schoolgirl, developed into
a sullen yet well-mannered teenager in high school—not an
athlete, and not terribly popular, but bookish, polite, extremely
intelligent. Then she was leaving for college in Columbus to
study English literature and writing. She wanted to become a
teacher and write books that might change the world.

And the world opened up to Gretchen in ways that
Cora found beyond her own understanding. After all, her
own dreams had been small and parochial—she knew that. A
home in the town she grew up in, marriage to her high school
sweetheart, children, and by now perhaps a comfortable
retirement with her husband—not much else had she wanted.
She hadn't felt the reach of bigger imaginings, those that might
beckon from realms far outside of her own. And well that she
hadn't, she knew also, because apparently God had seen fit to
stir up even her relatively modest designs, to relieve her of her
youthful fancies, and bring her here today as she was, old and
husbandless, still working on her feet for eight hours a day, but
yet—no, thank God—not childless. This much she did have, a
home and a child to love. And for that she would be grateful,
always grateful, in spite of the hardships.

How had Gretchen come by her large ideas? she

wondered. All those books she read, no doubt. And Lord knows what else they do and talk about on those college campuses. Cora didn't pretend to know about such things, wasn't even sure if she approved of it all. Politics, sex and philosophy, and the worldly religions—Cora didn't care to hear about it, but she knew that was what they were discussing in the classrooms and study lounges, the cafeteria and dormitories. Still, it had made her proud to know that Gretchen was absorbing so much while keeping her head about her, and that she would most probably go on to do great things, for that was what she had always hoped to do.

And now she was fulfilling her ambition, Cora proudly reflected, teaching the little ones in the community where she herself had grown up. She hoped Gretchen was satisfied, having avoided being corrupted by some of the more outrageous foolishness that occurs at university. Cora smiled uncertainly. Gretchen did seem to be happy in her work. It perhaps made it all worthwhile, she told herself.

Cora yawned in the darkness and heard the wind pick up outside her window. Time crept forward, slowly unfolding over the world like a warm tide. Sleep was a welcome relief from her anxious mental meanderings.

Down the hall, across the darkness and shadows and behind the painted wooden door of her bedroom, Gretchen was lying in bed as well, nestled in the folds of the blankets, her face warm against the pillow. Remembering, she was, also at that moment, days of several years past when she was still a college student, away from home and as yet unsure of her place in the world, hoping to find patterns of meaning behind the fog of uncertainty. She had sought it in familiar and pleasurable things, activities which, being in new and unfamiliar surroundings, she took pains to recreate in the image of what she remembered: the comfort, for instance, of sitting in a soft chair, wrapped in a blanket and drinking tea, reading Dickens, Ruskin or Carlyle in the warm yellow glow of her floor lamp. And she searched for significance in other realms, those yet foreign to her, but still exciting and ripe with possibilities in their newness.

Once, she recalled, not long after Invincibility's Great Jolt, when madness and irrational, panic-soaked paranoia seemed to reign over reason, she had boarded a chartered bus heading for Washington, D.C., a bus loaded with troubled critics of the regime, dissenters and impassioned ideologues, united to join a march near the National Mall against an impending U.S. invasion of Iraq. The bus left Columbus very early in the morning, and, though she knew no one on board, she felt at home among the passengers. They shared food and conversation, discussed concerns and hopes for the future, went over procedures to follow if anyone should be confronted by counter-demonstrators or the police, or even arrested. And when they arrived at their destination shortly before noon, she remembered vividly, it was freezing cold as they stepped off the bus in the shadow of the U.S. Capitol.

The size of the crowd was staggering to her. She had never before seen so many people in one place. Thousands upon thousands of people, young and old, of every imaginable race and nationality, many with children—they milled about in the frigid air, greeting each other, huddling, carrying signs and other props, some hawking buttons, literature, propaganda of varying perspectives. Gretchen looked around in wonder, not knowing which way to go at first. She spent an hour roaming the sloping lawn in front of the towering white marble dome, taking it all in as the fervent speeches bellowing from the stage echoed across the sea of people.

Eventually the call to march was made and the sea began to move. She found a place behind some young people carrying a large cloth banner stretched between long poles, next to a middle-aged man dressed as Uncle Sam on stilts. As she stood at a corner of the reflecting pool, waiting for a clearing in the crowd so she could move toward Independence Avenue, she felt a touch at her sleeve from just behind her on her left. She turned.

The young man was tall, slightly built and wearing a green windbreaker that seemed to Gretchen to offer little protection from the cold. Still, he showed no sign of discomfort. On the contrary, his intensity appeared to steel his movements and provide a sort of immunity from the elements. He held out a small folded newspaper in his ungloved hand.

"Would you like a *Socialist Worker?*" he asked politely, walking alongside her. "It has a story on the cover that exposes the lies surrounding this buildup to war." His face was pale and raw from the cold, edged by short brown whiskers on the sides and around the chin. His breathing produced vaporous puffs that partially fogged his round wire-rimmed glasses.

She looked at the paper, then at him. "You're a socialist?"

"Of course," he replied. "It's the capitalist drive for profits over people and the expansion into new markets that makes wars like this one inevitable. In this case, it's Big Oil's desire to control Middle East reserves. In Afghanistan it was securing a major natural gas pipeline route. Socialism offers the only real alternative to this craziness. Look, everyone here wants to avoid war. What they need to realize is that you can't end war until you end capitalism." He smiled at her. "Let me ask you a question. Do you consider yourself a capitalist?"

"Well, no. Not really. At least I don't think of myself that way."

"And yet you exist everyday to help perpetuate the capitalist system. It's not your fault. We all do to some extent. We can't help it. We support the very system that exploits us. We're tools of the system. But some of us are fighting to change that. If you really don't consider yourself a capitalist, then you should join us and help organize for a workers' revolution to end this insanity. Where are you from?" He spoke in a measured, confident manner that indicated he had had much practice in proselytizing.

"Columbus, Ohio."

"Are you a student?"

"Yes. I'm studying to be a teacher."

"Well, the teachers' unions have come out against this war. What we need is more union voices to push the anger toward the next step, a permanent end to the war-profiteering and a retooling of our economy to make it centered around meeting human needs, like education."

"So you really think there's going to be a socialist revolution in this country? Like a general strike or something?"

"I'll admit the conditions right now don't seem to favor it, but that can change very quickly. Once the people start to see the truth behind this war, and link it to the growing gap between rich and poor, the misallocation of resources, the devastation of our global environment—all of that—then who knows? It's the workers who produce the wealth that the capitalists then seize, but our role as producer gives us tremendous power, if we just learn how to use it to take control for the benefit of the people. That's a workers' revolution. The important thing is to organize and educate people for it now, so that when the time comes, the workers will be ready. It's happened before—the Paris Commune, the Bolsheviks in Russia. . ."

"I thought socialism was a thing of the past. Even the Soviet Union gave up on it." Gretchen found to her surprise that she enjoyed this argument of ideas. It seemed to fit the mood of the day, this discussion of new possibilities and paradigms that she had never before considered.

"The Soviet Union was never a true socialist system after Stalin betrayed the Revolution and created an authoritarian government, not a democratic one. It was more of a 'state capitalism,' where the government bureaucrats, not the people, control the economy, and the growth of capital remains the primary object, instead of the needs of the people. The same can be said of China, North Korea, Cuba—all the so-called socialist societies that the capitalists love to demonize. Besides, socialism cannot exist in a single country or even a few if the dominant global economic system remains capitalist. Marx and Engels understood that. Lenin and Trotsky understood that. Which is why they looked for socialism to begin in the most advanced countries and spread to the rest of the world. One reason the Russian Revolution ultimately failed is that it began in an underdeveloped country with the hope of spreading to Europe, but the governments of the more developed countries got together to crush it. If we can begin the revolution in this country, it will be much easier to organize an international movement. What we ultimately want is truly democratic government, on a global scale, but an economy that's controlled by the people, not by private corporations."

Gretchen stepped off the curb and found a place in the crowd, with the revolutionary evangelist continuing beside her. "That's asking people to make a huge change in their current thinking, don't you think?" she asked. "I'm not sure even I can imagine it."

"Sometimes people's willingness to embrace new ideas when their own future is at stake can surprise us." He turned excitedly to her. "Remember the protests in Seattle at the World Trade Organization meeting a few years ago? People had the right idea then—bring down the corporate goons who have been ripping off the poor for decades. Problem was, nobody was offering an alternative. Once you dismantle the current corrupt system, what do you replace it with? That's where socialists come in. We want an intelligently planned economy that puts priorities where they should be. We want to shut down the current system, but we're not anarchists."

He pointed out a group of young people with bandanas covering their faces, one of whom had climbed a light pole and was ostentatiously flourishing a ragged flag with a letter "A" enclosed in a circle. "See," he said, "they only know what they're against. They don't really know what they're for."

The pair turned a corner and became part of a colossal swell of people that began to ascend Capitol Hill, filling all lanes of Independence Avenue as police in riot gear stood shoulder-to-shoulder on the curbs to each side, silently watching. Spirited chants of "One! Two! Three! Four! We don't want your stinking war!" surrounded and enveloped the marchers, making attempts at conversation difficult. Gretchen was nearly knocked down by a woman attempting to maneuver the head of a large, grotesquely painted *papier-mâché* puppet that was on the verge of toppling over on her.

"Easy, comrade," the young man said to the woman, as he guided Gretchen out of harm's way. "We're not the enemy here."

Gretchen let out an embarrassed laugh and suddenly felt self-conscious. Not wanting to take up any more of the young man's time—he had stopped talking anyway and was surveying the crowd for other potential recruits—she gave him a dollar in return for a newspaper and promised to look up the local chapter of socialists when she returned to Columbus. She had a feeling of gratitude for his attention and willingness to talk to her. And for his sincerity. She was of a mind at this moment when sincerity meant something precious to her.

Overall, it had been a relatively peaceful march, and the turnout was magnificent, a massive demonstration of hundreds of thousands, all voicing their divergent viewpoints which nonetheless converged around a general opposition to U.S. warmongering. Sitting on the bus at the end of the day, exhausted yet exhilarated, waiting for the long drive back to Columbus,

Gretchen couldn't help but feel a muted depression, however, which would only expand in the coming months and years. For the day's effort would soon prove to have accomplished nothing really. One month later, the allied invasion of Iraq was underway, almost as if no opposition had been voiced at all. For Gretchen, it was her first lesson in the limits of human idealism. As the war, which became in later years an occupation, dragged on with no end in sight, she realized that things do not always of necessity work out for the best, that there was not a pre-mandated progressive march forward to a better future, that humankind did not always do the right thing in the end. No grand scheme, no guiding hand from on high. There was no cosmic statute that declared Good must always triumph over Evil. Sometimes things went terribly wrong, and making it all right again was not always possible. She never did look up the Columbus socialists, and it wasn't long before she gave up on politics altogether and merely refocused, with some regret, her attention on her studies, her teaching career, and the little things that made her happy—an engaging book, a warm chair, the glow of lamplight on winter evenings, and writing poems.

And as she lay in bed now, remembering, she felt she wanted more than ever a better life for her Aunt Cora, so that she would no longer have to rise on the frosted mornings well before the sun appeared, with little before her but to spend all day on her feet attending others. She wanted also to know that her own efforts with her students were not simply as snowflakes purposelessly drifting in the wind, inspired for a moment but doomed to melt on the asphalt and gurgle down the sewer drain. And she wanted a guarantee that the great works of humanity would be preserved and protected forever, that death would not interrupt a life that was yet to be fulfilled, that beauty and love would ultimately reign over ugliness and despair. These simple things she wanted, and yet she knew it was too much to expect. The universe was not so ordered. She saw that now.

Even the recent election, which had ignited a brief spark of hope that things might yet change for the better, failed to sustain a lasting fire of optimism in her. All was yet, and always would be, randomness and chaos, accident and contingency. And with these thoughts, she fell into sleep, drifting peacefully, into the dreams of the lost.

And across the hillside and down the slope among the lower-lying communities, Malcolm Peters rested his mind, sitting quietly in his darkened living room, staring out the window, hoping to discern a semblance of reassurance in the cold dormancy that lay outside, enveloped in blackness. He could hear the wind hissing, but saw only the empty, snow-frozen field that glimmered softly on the adjacent property, and beyond, barely visible, the slumbering, black-windowed house of his nearest neighbor. His thoughts were again of Anna and what she would have to say about his current state, viewing it with the broad, all-encompassing perspective regarding trivial human matters which the dead must possess, if indeed they can be said to possess anything at all.

"After a lifetime of enduring the doings of deceitful people," she might say, "now you decide to take it upon yourself to tilt at undefined windmills?"

"That's not true, Anna. I did fight back before. You know I did. I just never won."

"And what do you expect to win now? To say you righted a small wrong? What is your cause, Malcolm? What battle are you waging?"

"Anna, I love you. But there are no small wrongs. Small wrong or big wrong. They all offend morality. I can't abide it."

"And yet abide we must, Malcolm. We all must abide. . . "

She would indeed say that, he affirmed. That was Anna, abiding with limitless patience the vicissitudes of the world and its inhabitants. He closed his eyes and imagined then the procession of the many dead before him, the recent loved ones and the ancients, those he had known and those he did not know, and also his father and mother. He saw his mother, with arms outstretched to embrace a suffering world with her love, speaking in a wordless language, with a soundless voice. "Child, child, child," she was saying, "What dreams do you dream, you who yet breathe the breath of the living, while we who are dust dream our dreams of eternity? With what hopes do you wake when the softness of morning smiles down upon your sweet face? I am your mother who loved you. Do you remember?"

"I remember, Ma. I can't forget." Silently he mouthed the words.

"You remember I tried to teach you the ways of the world. How to repay acts of cruelty and unkindness with understanding and forgiveness. Hatred and deceit with loving surrender. Yet you chose your own way, and lived a life burdened with worry and sorrow. Have you lost all hope?"

"Hope is a currency I have little truck with. I know the ways of the world, Ma."

"And on what foundation is your knowledge grounded? You temper your certainty with doubt, is it not so?"

"Yes."

"And your convictions are frayed and torn by abuse. . . "

"Mmm, yes."

"Have faith then. Above all, Malcolm, this is what you must do—you must remember your Mother in your prayers—"

"You know I don't pray, Ma."

"And your father here as well, who loved you as I did. Do you remember?"

The edges of his mouth curled slightly upward, his lips moving soundlessly. "I remember you, Pops. I remember you always liked it when I called you Pops."

He could see the old man smiling, saying, "Yes I did,

son. I liked it a lot. You know, Pops—the real Pops—he was your namesake. The way he blew that horn was somethin' smooth and tasty as melted butterscotch. The way he wowed the people just made you cry. A real showman, yes sir, a fine entertainer. Knew what the people wanted and, my lord, he gave it to 'em. That's why I named you after him."

"But I didn't want that name, Pops. Why'd you give me his name? Sure he could play, but what's that to me? I always pretended my middle name came from Joe Louis, a real fighter."

"Well, it's your name to lie about as you please."

"Pops, why didn't you fight back? Why did you always accommodate?"

"What do you know about accommodation? You never accommodated? You don't know what it was like. I had to earn a living, and if the big boss in Washington said he would give me a job so long as I caused him no trouble, then by God that's what I would do so you and your sister wouldn't have to be raised in no sweltering Alabama cotton field like I was. I couldn't be chasing noble causes and scarin' up the white folk like you did. You had the luxury to dabble with your radical politics because I sacrificed that luxury for myself. And what all did it get you anyway? They still conscripted your ass and sent you off to fight in their war. They put you in that classroom for thirty years and told you to teach those kids who never knew nothin' but society's pig slop and then expected you to make them unlearn their oppression like it was just a bad habit. And now you live there in that town full of white folks, the only lonesome Negro for miles around, making nice with everyone like they was family. Do you know what people say about you behind your back? Do you know what they think about you in the back corners of their minds?"

"I know, Pops. But what I'm dealing with now is bigger than that. I'm nearing the end of the line and here I've been fighting and I don't know for what, or against what. Nothing seems to makes sense. And see this cat died recently—I guess I could say he was a friend, or an acquaintance—but in any case he was a decent guy. And he died strangely—"

"I know."

"—and it seems that people involved in this are not what they pretend to be—"

"Ain't it the same the world over?"

"—and there's something fishy about the whole thing. I know it's insignificant in the big scheme of things, but I'm bothered—personally discontented—because I want to do the right thing. . . "

"And yet the right thing sometimes just refuses to be done. Ain't it so, Malcolm?"

As his father faded from view, Malcolm sat quietly in the darkness, turned his head to look at the frozen landscape framed by the window, felt the chill diffusing through it. The emptiness permeated his skin and hollowed out his insides. In his mind he replayed the record of his life. There in the dark he summoned up images from the past—scenes of his birthplace in a rural Alabama sharecropper's shack; the family journey soon after to the nation's capital with promises of good government jobs and a perhaps less overbearing Jim Crow; his rebellious boyhood on the streets of D.C.; his draft notice from Uncle Sam foretelling a nightmarish tour of duty defending liberty in a foreign land he had never heard of. On his return he discovered that the scales had fallen from his eyes and he saw his life as it was. The world around him was in upheaval and he felt helplessly carried along like a cork in a sea swell. Yet he was full-grown in awareness and determined now to immerse himself fervidly in the surrounding storm.

The night progressed in a dead calm. He continued to sit in his chair, staring out the window at the timestopped stillness, remembering now the riots that had convulsed his own

home city in the nineteen-sixties following the assassination
of Reverend King. What happened, how it happened, why
it happened were beyond all understanding, as all that was
happening then sped past in manic blurs of running madness.
He had not been home when it happened; he was on the other
side of the world fighting in a different war zone, an overblown
police action staged in waterlogged rice paddies and under
steaming jungle canopies. But he saw the aftermath, and heard
the stories and watched the newsreels. His old neighborhood
around 14th and U Streets lying in charred rubble heaps, the
white National Guard troops standing with weapons at the
ready, glaring at the black residents—these were images that
laid a hurt on him far deeper and longer-lasting than any he
brought back with him from his soldiering odyssey.

He enrolled in D.C. Teachers College, joined the local
chapter of the Black Panther Party, committed himself to the
Ten Point Program and the pursuit of revolutionary action
manifested through free breakfast programs, organizing in
poor communities, and devoted study of the history of militant
people's movements. Not out of hatred for white people, he told
himself, but out of love for black people. Coming by his newly
found radicalism was not difficult. The pace of events that were
thrust upon him and his comrades saw to that. The assassination
of Fred Hampton by the Chicago police, the murder of George
Jackson at San Quentin, the Attica inmate uprising, the police
raid on the chapter office in D.C., the ongoing escalation of
war, and the relentless, ever-present burden of impoverishing
racism all whetted his enthusiasm for unflinching rebellion
against established oppression, what Huey P. Newton had
called "Revolutionary Suicide."

And then he met Anna. Unlike him, she was unworried
by an urge to dissent. She'd wanted a stable home and a family
with Malcolm, little more. She acted as a rudder to his wildly
veering passions. And she encouraged him to focus exclusively

on his teacher education and effect the revolution he desired through mentoring the young people. With her gentle nudging, he eventually transitioned from the streets to the classroom, and from a new attitude of fostering change "from within, not outside, the system," as Anna put it, he watched as the radical movement concomitantly disintegrated around him.

Rousing himself from his quiet reverie, Malcolm suddenly became aware again of his present surroundings. The room was beginning to lighten, ever so slightly taking on the bluish-gray tinge of emerging winter dawn. Outside, the overcast sky slowly shed its deep shroud of blackness, giving way to a gloomy pall that portended a day of little promise. He rose from the chair with a heavy sigh, and Maggie, who had been snoring peacefully at his feet the entire night, got up and stretched, then headed drowsily for the kitchen with her tail wagging in anticipation. *This is not right*, he thought to himself as he followed her. Something had to be done, he was sure now. The voices of the past had returned to their eternal slumber, but the future still lay ahead. And so forward he went, still uncertain of his path, yet determined to follow it where it would lead. *And so it goes*, he thought. And so it went.

CHAPTER TWENTY

And so it happened that several days later, Malcolm found himself, on the evening of the first Saturday in March, sitting at his desk in the hallway, picking up the telephone receiver and dialing the number for Ruth Ingram of Weehawken, New Jersey, the unearthing of which his newfound skills at internet searching had proven most helpful in accomplishing. After three rings, the line was picked up. "Hello?" It was a female voice, sounding confident and self-possessed.

"Uh, yes, hello. I'm trying to reach Ms. Ruth Ingram?"

"This is she."

"Uh, Ms. Ingram, my name is Malcolm Peters. I'm sorry to bother you like this, but I had read about you in the newspaper article about the death of your ex-husband—"

"Yes." The voice stiffened, became a touch suspicious.

Malcolm said hastily, "I'm sorry for your loss—"

"It wasn't my loss. We had been divorced for quite some time. Now what can I do for you?"

"Well, you see, I live in the same town where his brother, Frank Allerton, lived. Frank was a friend of mine. And as you may know, there have been some questions about his death last November."

The voice relaxed slightly. "Oh, well, I'm sorry for *your* loss, Mr. Peters. As you know from that article, the police are still looking into the situation. Or at least they claim to be. I thought it was quite unfortunate how they contributed—in my opinion—to Jonathan's death. He was already very upset about his brother's suicide, and then to be suspected of having something to do with it was just devastating for him."

"I understand. I read that he said he was not in Ohio when Frank died."

"That's right," she said definitively. "He was not."

"Well, could I take a few minutes of your time to tell you what happened here during that time? It's all very strange and confusing, and you might like to know, because it seems to tie in somehow with what happened out there."

And so it went that Malcolm and Ruth talked briefly over the phone, after which she suggested that they correspond further by email, each one laying down the events as he or she saw them transpire. And through this process, as he later told Gretchen, they hoped to bring some enlightened clarity to the mysteries that haunted both parties.

And Malcolm related Ruth's story to Gretchen, there in the Sunnyland Diner over coffee, one cold and cloudy Sunday afternoon a week later. He said she spoke about how she and Jonathan Allerton had met back in college. She was an undergraduate and he was a graduate student at Rutgers University. And they were together as a couple for a few years while they were students, then they got married shortly after he finished his degree, she having already graduated and begun working. "Only it was a little rocky along the way," Malcolm told Gretchen. "She says she was young and foolish and flirty, you know, and, well, she wasn't always faithful to him. Her husband, she says, was a decent man, but she fooled around on him, before and during the marriage, with another grad student who worked with her husband, guy named Jake Reese Hart. Funny name. And he was a weird sort of spaced-out cat too, very smart but not always focused, and he eventually dropped out of school without getting his degree.

"Well, time went on and Ruth and her husband Jonathan settled in with their lives and their own separate careers—she as accountant for some place that does sets for Broadway shows and he with being a chemistry professor. But this guy Jake kind of continues coming in and out of the picture, and Ruth goes back and forth with him on the sly. She feels real guilty about it but she can't manage to quit him." He paused, gave a tilt of the head, as if considering. He went on: "Ruth also kind of justified it in her own mind by saying she suspected her husband of fooling around too. Who knows? Anyway, years go by like this. This Jake character is drifting around north Jersey, doing odd jobs, musical gigs—he apparently plays jazz piano pretty well—living in various places, popping in and out of their lives. He kind of maintained an acquaintance with Ruth's husband—did I mention they both worked in the same chemistry lab during grad school?—but she says she knew that he—her husband—was kind of getting tired of Jake, and his lack of ambition, sometimes showing up to ask for a loan or such. She doesn't think her husband had any real certainty about their affair, but she started to worry that he was getting suspicious. Anyway, this sort of thing eventually poisons a marriage, and it got to a point where they separated for a while, at his insistence, and this kind of shook her up. But she went and rented her own apartment, feeling really bad about this whole thing with Jake, and wanting to end it somehow, because she knows he's not good for her. And she and Jake went off to some lake resort in the Poconos that summer. Seems he planned this with the thought that this was gonna be the start of something solid between them finally, but she says she was so ate up with guilt that she told him right there that it was over—she washed her hands of the whole affair. So she went back to Jersey alone, he just stayed on in Pennsylvania, and she didn't hear from him again. He must've took it pretty hard." Malcolm paused again, looked out the window. "She and her husband got together again for a while, but it was all over really and he finally told her he wanted a divorce. She moved all her stuff out of the house, went to Weehawken. That was about ten years ago."

Gretchen watched him for a moment as he looked back at her. "That's so sad, don't you think?" she said plaintively.

Malcolm turned his gaze from the window back to her. "Yeah, well, then move it ahead ten years and it gets real interesting. Seems last summer when her husband—ex-husband—retired from his university job, he started trying to reconnect with her. Now remember, they hadn't had anything to do with each other for ten years. So then he called her a few times, said he wanted to get back on a friendly basis with her. Didn't want them to die enemies—her words. She thinks he was feeling time slipping away, the usual sort of regrets we start to feel as we get older." He smiled a little. "So she says fine. They talk some, catch up on each other's lives. Turns out *he's* been in touch with Jake. They've been getting reacquainted, this after Jake had been out of the picture for a while. Jake is still the same, slumming around aimlessly, looking for his next break. Now mind you, he's a very smart guy; just can't seem to get it together, you know. And these folks are in their sixties now—Jake and Jonathan.

"So Ruth and her ex-husband go out together a few times. Just friendly dates, nothing serious. Neither one of them is interested in that. So here's the weird thing. They're out at a restaurant one night in November, a week or so before Thanksgiving, she thinks. Later, when she gets home—and she's alone now—she sees she has a message on her home answering machine from someone who doesn't identify himself, but she knows it's Jake. He says he just called to tell her he made it. Made it where? She doesn't know. She checks the number with 'star 69;' it's a cell phone, but of course she can't tell where he is calling from. Now this just happens to be at the time that Frank was being visited by his brother. We all met the guy, only how could it have been his brother when his brother was having dinner that night with Ruth in New Jersey? And this so-called brother was here when Frank died, or at least just before he died. Then he disappeared. Jonathan Allerton later gives the police his statement saying he wasn't in Ohio then, and Ruth corroborates it. So are they believable? If they are, who was the guy we met here who claimed to be Frank's brother?"

He paused, looking expectantly at Gretchen. "Maybe it was this man Jake," she offered. "The message he left her was to say he was here, maybe?"

"Hmmm. Well, that's what Ruth says. But why would he have taken the trouble to visit Frank out here, pretending to be his brother? I guess it's conceivable that he could get away with it, since nobody in town, including Frank, had seen him or heard from him for nearly fifty years. But why would he do it?"

"Did Ruth ever call back that number? The one she thought was Jake?"

"Yes, but not right away. She didn't want to speak to Jake again. But after all these suspicions came up over Frank's death and Jonathan's possible connection to it, she started to wonder, and she did call. She used a public pay phone so the person who answered wouldn't know it was her. Well, his service had been cut off. This was just a few weeks before Jonathan died."

He looked out the window again. "The thing is, Ruth says that her husband—ex-husband—was actually planning to visit his brother for real. He told her as much when they were communicating last November. Just like he was sort of reconciling with her toward what he saw was the end of his life, seems he also wanted to do the same with his brother. She says he really held a grudge against Frank—blaming him for their father's death long ago—and shortly after that was when he left home and never returned. I guess he was figuring now that forty-seven years of the silent treatment was long enough. Even sent Frank a letter to that effect. But he never heard back from him. You can imagine that Frank suddenly dying—from a suicide, just as he was hoping they'd reconnect—would've really tore him up inside."

Malcolm stopped again and faced Gretchen directly. "Why would Frank kill himself when he knew his brother was coming to visit?"

"But his brother was already here," Gretchen replied. "Or at least someone claiming to be his brother. Maybe Frank had doubts about him. Maybe being visited by someone he wasn't sure was really his brother, in addition to having received that letter, were confusing to Frank. It would have been to anyone. But then, like you said, why kill yourself?"

"Yeah, why?" He was silent for a moment, thinking.

They both looked at each other, seeming to come to similar conclusions which they left unsaid. Gretchen was weighing the implications of Malcolm's narrative. Finally she asked, "Shouldn't you go to the police?"

Malcolm shrugged and pursed his lips. "There's no evidence for any suspicions I might have. And besides, they're not going to be interested my opinions." He leaned back in the booth and rubbed his hands over his head. "You know, this whole affair just gets more and more complicated."

He leaned forward and stared straight at Gretchen, questioningly. "Colonel Haygood told me Frank changed his will just a few days before he died, naming his brother as the main beneficiary. He doesn't know why. It was a substantial amount of money. Now with his brother dead too, I wonder where all of it goes. There's no one else left in that family."

"Maybe his ex-wife will get everything," Gretchen said musingly.

"Mmmm, yeah. Wouldn't that be funny. Anyway, it's all on hold for now till they clear up the police investigation." Malcolm then lowered his head and raised his eyes to Gretchen uncertainly. "And another thing," he said, watching her. "She, uh, invited me to come out and see her. . . "

Gretchen started back in surprise. "In New Jersey?"

"Yeah. I was a little startled myself. But we had been talking a few times on the phone, and by email. She said if we met face-to-face we could discuss things more freely, and she seemed to hint that there were some things she wanted to show me."

"I'm sure," Gretchen replied with a sly grin. "You'd better be careful, Malcolm. She doesn't sound like the most scrupulous person in the world."

Malcolm shifted uncomfortably and said, "I know. It's just that there's still so many questions about this whole thing that are unanswered. I don't know why, but I feel like I need to get to the bottom of it all, for my own peace of mind." He shrugged. "I dunno. Maybe I want to do it for Frank. He wasn't such a bad guy. I think he deserves to have all the questions answered. Besides, I could use a quick getaway from this place for a couple days. Maybe the weather's better there."

"I doubt it. But it does sound like you're going a little stir crazy here in the country. Maybe you do need a little city life to restart your engines. I know I'd take a vacation from here if I could." Then she anticipated his question, adding with a smile, "And, yes, I'll be glad to take care of Maggie."

CHAPTER TWENTY-ONE

When Malcolm's plane arrived in Newark, the afternoon was damp, overcast, and suffused with a lingering, late-winter cold. With only an overnight bag to carry, he took a cab directly from the airport to the address in Weehawken that Ruth Ingram had provided. It was a white two-story, slant-roofed house, sandwiched snuggly between its neighboring residences, with a large front porch and steps that descended onto the sidewalk. As he mounted the steps, a nervous trepidation overcame him, and he paused for a moment, staring anxiously at the front windows, looking for signs of life. *What am I doing here?* he wondered. His gaze went up and down the quiet block, lined with more attached houses and a few cars parked in the otherwise deserted street. He considered turning around and going back home, but just then the front door opened, and a well-groomed, dark-haired woman in her late fifties stood looking down at him with an expression of cautious welcome. He could see she must have displayed at one time an abundance of youthful prettiness, which by now had matured into a settled poise less reliant on outward features, yet bolstered by a projected inner radiance.

"Mr. Malcolm Peters?" she asked.

He smiled and nodded, then with one last look around him, ascended the steps into the open door. "Hello, Ms. Ingram."

"Do come in," she replied in a business-like tone, making way for him to enter. "And please call me Ruth."

"And, uh, you should call me Malcolm."

As she shut the door behind him, he saw that the interior was furnished in a tasteful old-fashioned décor, with delicate lace curtains filtering the diffused afternoon light through the front windows. It was warm inside, and she took his coat as his eyes passed over the polished hardwood floor to an area where the living room furniture—two brown armchairs and a brown leather couch—sat upon a large mauve rug, arranged in a semi-circle in front of and facing the fireplace. A small fire was burning, throwing off a glow that was reflected in the varnished surface of a bare mahogany coffee table, the center of the sitting area. A shaded floor lamp next to one of the chairs added the only other illumination to the fading light from the windows.

"To tell you the truth, Malcolm, I expected you to be, well, white." She smiled coyly, then appeared to be alarmed at her own forwardness. "I hope that doesn't offend you. It's just—"

"Oh no," he said quickly to dispel any awkwardness. "I understand. I am sort of an oddball in Vernen." He added, "But I've only been living there for two years. I retired from Washington, D.C. I was a teacher there for thirty years."

"I see. Well, please make yourself comfortable. I see you brought some luggage. You're welcome to stay here for the night. I have an extra room—"

"No, thank you. I have a room at a hotel in town. I just thought I should come here first to see you, but I'll go there and check in later tonight."

She showed what seemed to Malcolm to be more than a little interest. "Oh. What hotel?" she inquired.

"Just a few blocks away, toward the river. I fly back in the morning. Can't leave my dog too long. She gets to missing me."

Ruth stood there for a moment, eyeing him curiously. Then she said, "Well, I can fix us some coffee, and would you like something to eat?"

"Some coffee would be fine."

She went into the kitchen while Malcolm sat in one of the armchairs upholstered in soft brown fabric. He heard running water as she called out to him, "I know this is strange for both of us." He leaned over in his chair to get a glimpse of her standing over the kitchen sink, attentively scrubbing her hands. "Jonathan and his brother are distant parts of my past—a past I'd just as soon forget about now if I could."

"You'd never met Frank, is that right?"

"No. But I did hear enough of him from Jonathan. Even though he never spoke to him, he certainly talked enough about him to me." She scooped some grounds into a coffee maker, poured in the water, and plugged the machine into an outlet above the counter. "I think he still maintained a desire to reunite with his brother, but he was rather weak-willed when it came to revisiting his past. He could never bring himself to do it."

She returned to the living room and elegantly seated herself on the leather couch. The gurgling coffee maker resounded languidly from the kitchen, filling the air with its acrid, steaming aroma.

"And Jonathan never went back to Ohio?" Malcolm inquired casually. He watched Ruth closely when she answered. He was beginning to feel comfortable enough in the unfamiliar house to remember his purpose in coming, and he did not want his mission lost to any inattention on his part.

"No." Ruth sighed and shook her head. "He never did."

Staring now, focusing in on her face as the intensity of the noises from the brewing coffee increased, he asked another question. "What kind of car did Jonathan drive? I mean what color?"

She stared back at him as if lost in thought, her face like a photograph. Then her expression relaxed and she smiled a little, acquiescing to her compromised status. "All right, Malcolm. Yes, I haven't been quite honest. I just gave you a standard reply to the police interrogations, the veracity of which doesn't really have any bearing on the tragedy that occurred out there. Jonathan did in fact drive out to see his brother a few weeks before Frank died, but he never saw him. Another manifestation of his lack of will. He drove all the way out there and parked outside of Frank's house. But he lost his nerve and never got out of the car. He just sat there looking at the house, then turned around and drove back home. Can you believe it? I hardly could when he told me about it afterwards, but it sounds so typical of the kind of person Jonathan was." The sounds of the coffee maker died down and she got up to go to the kitchen. "And to answer the actual question you asked," she called back as she walked, "he drove a green Civic."

Malcolm pondered this as he sat waiting for Ruth to return. When she did, carrying a tray with two full coffee mugs and two small cups made of cut glass and filled with cream and sugar, he asked, "Would you say that Jonathan had a sort of. . . um. . . Santa Claus appearance?"

She laughed. "Is that how you saw him? Yes, I suppose you could describe him that way, a bit on the heavy side, though not all that fat. He grew a big horrible beard after we divorced. His way, I suppose, of reinventing himself."

"I didn't see him. Someone I know did." He thanked Ruth for the coffee and sipped it carefully. "That's an odd thing to do, though. All that driving, and for what?"

"Well, as I said, it fit right into Jonathan's character. I believe I've told you, he had informed me that he'd written a letter to Frank sometime in October to try to reconcile with him. It took him a while to trace Frank's address, as he had moved from the house they'd grown up in, but he still resided in the same town. He waited about a week after sending the letter and when he didn't hear anything back from Frank he just decided to go and drive out there. I told him, 'Give Frank a little time to respond. Getting a letter from you out of the blue like that after so many years probably was quite a shock to his system. Give him some time to get his head on straight and I'm sure he'll respond to you.' But he couldn't wait. He did this a lot. Would get an impulsive urge in him and follow it, only to chicken out at the last minute, in this case after driving all the way across Pennsylvania." She paused to put cream and sugar in her coffee. "But I can tell you for certain, Malcolm, that he was not there when Frank died, and he had nothing to do with it. When the police called to tell him, it really threw him off kilter. He was very depressed."

"Then who was it that was with him the week he died? The guy I met. Do you know?"

She brought the coffee cup to her lips and sipped. "No," she said, putting the cup down again. She stared at him with an intense sincerity. "I really don't."

Outside the house, the afternoon moved forward with a dissipation of cloud cover. Presently the room they occupied lightened as the pitch of the cold sunlight through the lace curtains declined and its hue took on a rosy pink. The two finished their coffees over polite conversation that masked an undercurrent of expectancy on both sides. Malcolm became increasingly uncertain about his presence in this strange woman's living room. The nature of the information she had so far provided him hardly warranted his making the trip all the way out here; she could just as easily have told him these things over the phone. As he was deliberating over a graceful way to announce his exit, she said, "Malcolm, if you'll wait here, I have something I want to show you."

She left the room and went upstairs. Malcolm stared into the fire, watching the logs crackle and crumble into orange embers. He did not notice Ruth's return until she appeared before him cradling a small item in her hands with great care.

As she approached, he discerned that it was a small, darkly stained wooden box, hand-carved and painted with quaint floral designs. She stopped and held it out for him to take. He saw that it had a hinged lid, and on opening it discovered that it was a music box, which immediately commenced to play a lovely outpouring of tinkling notes flowing in a pattern of ascending and descending arpeggios that filled the silence of the room with melancholy. She went back to the brown leather couch and sat down.

"Beethoven,'" she said to his inquiring look, speaking over the music. "Do you like it?"

"It's nice, yes," he answered, puzzled.

"Look on the inside of the lid."

He did, and saw that a small white index card was taped there, with a short handwritten missive printed in black ink.

He looked at her. "Read it," she said.

He did so aloud:

> If you want to be a builder, be quite sure of your tools,
> If you want to climb a mountain, be mindful of the slope,
> And if, perhaps, the principled life is what you seek to lead,
> Base your principles on what's real, not simply what you hope.

He looked up at her. She smiled.

"Curious, isn't it? He gave it to me the last night we were together. The night I told him it was over between us. Funny sort of gift—a music box that plays 'Für Elise,' with that very strange bit of advice he composed taped on the inside. What do you think he meant by it?"

"I have no idea," he replied cautiously.

"Oh, I think you would understand if you thought about it." She leaned back on the couch and smiled. "You play the part well, Malcolm, but there's no denying it. You're just like the rest of us, in spite of your attempts to isolate yourself. You want to be different, but you can't. The fact that you're here proves it." She leaned forward. "Why did you come all the way out here just on my request? I mean, a woman you claim to not even know?"

"I don't follow you, Ruth." He tilted his head inquiringly. The music box began to wind down, the melody slowing, struggling to play out a few more notes before finally expiring into silence.

"All this about Jonathan and Frank, and Jake and me—"

"Jake?" He said it abruptly, with a tinge of alarm, as if she had guessed at some secret thought that he wasn't even sure of himself.

"Yes, the one who gave me that music box, of course. Remember I told you about him over the phone." She paused, looking at him expectantly, then an expression of realization came over her face. "Oh, maybe you thought I meant Jonathan gave it to me. Well, it doesn't really matter. Our lives have been tangled up with one another for so long, it's almost as if one couldn't exist without the others. And anyway you're a part of it now. You're the successor." She laughed at his obvious confusion. "Oh, don't pretend you didn't know. Although I suppose I didn't know myself for the longest time, or maybe I knew but didn't want to acknowledge it." She leaned forward and her voice took on a serious tone. "Jake, whom I've told you about, has always been a troubled soul. Talented, but troubled. He never could accept his lot in life, though it was mostly of his own making. And he hated Jonathan for his successes: with his career, with his relations with people, and—" she paused and looked beyond Malcolm for a moment, "—with me. His envy was far beyond what could be considered healthy. Eventually he responded to it by self-delusion. By, in essence, convincing himself that he had what he could never really have. Do you understand?"

Malcolm set the music box down on the coffee table and said slowly, "No, not really. . . "

She sighed deeply and said, "He became what he never was. He took what was never his. And he lied. All throughout he lied, and people believed him." Ruth stared full-faced into Malcolm's eyes and said quietly, "And now, Mr. Peters, what is it you want to become? And what is it you want to possess? And what lies are you willing to tell to get them?"

They looked at each other for a long time. Presently, she got up, retrieved the music box from the table and returned to her seat, speaking as she did so. "I know now what he meant by having principles based in what's real, not simply what we hope is real. Do you understand that? Do you want to live a principled life? And where are your principles based? In your memories of the past? We're all bound together by common things: by music, our love of a song, or a poem, some small trifle that takes on an enormous depth of meaning that we have no understanding of, yet we know it must be significant because it draws us in so powerfully. Why are you so driven to solve this mystery concerning Frank's death? Why did you in fact travel all the way out here just on the invitation of a woman you didn't even know? What do you hope to find? What is it *you* want to possess? Perhaps it's me, mmm?"

She got up again and approached him. She settled herself minx-like upon the arm of his chair and, leaning forward, seductively wrapped her right arm around the back of his neck. Malcolm sat frozen, wanting to move yet unable to pull away from the hand that rubbed his shoulder with provocative intent. She brought her lips close to his ear and whispered, "Jake has become Jonathan, Mr. Peters. And you have become Jake."

The words chilled him. He wanted to reply to her in the negative, to tell her that she was mistaken, that her inferences about his motivations were in error. True, he had entered into a world of which he knew little, but he had done so with the purest of intentions. He wanted to find the truth behind Frank's death, to right a morally offensive wrong, as he saw it. He *was* living the principled life, and his principles were rock-solid and correct. He knew this, was assured of this, and he wanted to tell her of his assurance. But speak it he could not.

Malcolm got up quickly and began to walk to the front door. "I'd better be going, Ms. Ingram." He picked up his travel bag from the floor and opened the closet to retrieve his coat. As he did so, he noticed a small brown valise pushed back in the corner of the closet, with a Greyhound identification tag tied to the handle. Upon the tag was scrawled Ruth's address. It struck him as odd; Ruth didn't seem like the bus-traveling type. Her tastes were more refined. But his mind quickly discarded the anomaly as he made haste to remove himself from his present predicament. "Thanks for your hospitality."

Ruth remained seated and turned to watch him. "You'll get what you want, Mr. Peters. You'll wring the truth out of the whole conundrum. I know you will. But I'll get what I want as well. And I believe you'll help me. Your vaunted idealism can't match the forces of nature, Mr. Peters. In the end you'll have to give in. There are concessions to be made."

He opened the front door, then paused and turned back to look at her one more time. She had a devouring, animalistic aspect to her that frightened him. She stared straight at him, lips moist and parted, her body alluringly posed on the chair with her hand softly stroking her cheek, moving down to caress her throat and then to methodically undo the top buttons of her blouse. He turned away in a hurry and went out the door, into the cold still twilight. He rushed headlong as fast as he could toward his hotel.

CHAPTER TWENTY-TWO

Malcolm Peters walked briskly with his suitcase in hand down the street to his hotel, some ten blocks away. His path was a descent downhill toward the waterfront, and the chill cut through his heavy coat as he watched the gleam from the fading sun behind him reflected in the empty windows of the buildings he passed. *A frozen wasteland,* he remarked to himself, the darkening sky falling before him like a colossal drapery. The hard, unyielding concrete beneath his footfalls jangled his teeth. *This is like a bad movie,* he thought. Then he corrected himself. *No, it isn't. It's like a play; it's three-dimensional, and the actors have moved aside to allow the audience to step up and take over the stage. That's me. I was the audience, but I'm not anymore. I'm deep in it now.*

The people in his path moved past him like ghosts, hunched and mumbling, eyeing him with cold detachment. Ruth's unsettling behavior moments before had shocked him with the realization that he had fallen into a separate underworld from which it might not be possible to escape. She seemed to be telling him something that he may have already known—about her ex-husband, her ex-lover, and about Malcolm himself. By attempting to assume responsibility for righting a terrible wrong, he had stepped into an unmediated arena wherein the forces of human vice had free reign. No honest conviction could survive in such a climate.

His ruminations ended as he now found himself, weary and cold-beat, standing before the majestic ten-story redbrick hotel that was to be his lodging for the night. His eyes followed the looming façade upward past the wildly fluttering flag hanging from a pole that jutted at an upward angle from the brick face, farther still past the gilded and glinting windows that allowed no view of their inner goings-on, finally on to the dusky sky beyond the roof. He breathed deeply and ascended the smooth marble steps, passed through the brass-framed revolving door, then stood for a moment to take in the warmth of the lobby and absorb the peaceful ambience that suggested sanctuary from the pursuing darkness outside. There was a calm, whispering sound throughout, and something else. Hearing faint piano music, he looked around and traced its source to a room off to the distant right, what appeared to be a restaurant and lounge bustling with dinner-hour guests. He turned back and approached the reception desk to check in, then rode the elevator to the fourth floor to find his room.

Once inside, with the door closed, Malcolm set down his suitcase and hung his coat in the closet. He lay down on the bed and closed his eyes with a weary sigh. He wanted to go to sleep, to not have to think anymore. It was too exhausting. He wondered if his journey to the east had been a mistake. He felt no closer to resolving the enigma that had led him to this place; was not even certain as to the question he was trying to answer.

Presently he rose and sat on the edge of the bed, gazing into the large mirror over the oak dresser before him. He wondered at the reflection that stared back at him. The face was changed, appeared to be more drawn, more timeworn, than he had previously imagined. The once angular, purposefully set features now looked sagging and limp, compromised and almost lifeless. He thought about going down to the lounge to get something to eat, although he wasn't hungry. He resolved to do so anyway.

He washed up in the bathroom and left the room,

heading for the elevator. The hallway was eerily quiet, the elevator empty. Stepping into the lobby on the ground floor, he followed the still audible piano music into the restaurant and went straight to the bar. He ordered a neat bourbon and sat absently sipping his drink, occasionally reaching his hand into a bowl of sugared peanuts. A feeling of settled quiet now took hold of him, and Malcolm casually scanned the room as the indistinct murmur of conversation and the muted tinkling of piano music and silverware on ceramic plates mellowed in his ears. The place had a curiously subdued atmosphere, lit by somber red glowing bulbs in wrought-iron sconces on the wall and table candles surrounded in red glass.

Soon his gaze settled upon the grand piano across the room and the man seated at it, absorbed in his playing. Malcolm was lifting his glass to his lips, looking at the piano player, when he froze, open-mouthed, and the intensity of his stare suddenly deepened. His eyes narrowed and he leaned forward slightly, slowly setting his glass down on the bar but keeping his eyes upon the man at the piano, an elderly white-haired man dressed in a slightly worn yet dapper formal black suit and tie. A revelation of shocked incredulity swept across his mind like a fast-moving train, and his lips formed words which his voice could scarcely utter.

"I'll. . . be. . . damned," he whispered in rank dismay. "I'll be god-damned!"

It can't be! he declared to himself. *It can't! But is it?*

He eased himself off the barstool, leaving his drink, and slowly wended his way through the tables toward the piano player. He stopped a few feet away and stood before the man, the large piano between the two, and he continued staring and looking as if he was deciding something of great importance in his mind. The man played on and took no apparent notice until he had finished the song. Then, amid a smattering of polite applause from the diners, he looked up at Malcolm, sat erect with his hands on his knees, and smiled pleasantly. Malcolm self-consciously, almost timidly, stepped forward and spoke.

"Excuse me, but I feel like I've met you before." He stood there awkwardly scrutinizing the other's face as if mysteriously drawn in to the pale translucence of the flaccid and folded skin. "Yes," he was saying dreamily, squinting, "the beard is gone and the hair trimmed and the demeanor is slightly altered, but the black eyes and the coloring and the build—" he ran his eyes down his subject and back up to take in fully the seated frame, then returned his attention to the face, "—and especially the slightly crooked nose. . . it's all still the same. I know you."

"And I know you!" the man replied with exaggerated jauntiness. "You're a lover of good music, who has no compunction about playing benefactor for the evening to a humble yet sincere practitioner of the art." He reached for the empty tip jar on top of the piano and held it out to Malcolm with an expression of mock humility. "How about the first tip of the evening?"

Malcolm, taken aback slightly, checked his initial forwardness. "I'm sorry," he said demurely. "My name's Malcolm Peters. Surely I met you at Frank Allerton's house in Ohio last November? You're his brother, Jonathan."

The man remained seated as he listened, then shook his head thoughtfully and replied, "Mmmm, no. No, that wouldn't be me. My name's Jack the Piano Man." He played an ascending arpeggio on the keyboard with a flourish, then looked up at Malcolm with an expectant smile.

Certainty and doubt were doing battle in Malcolm's mind as he stared down at this familiar yet altered personage before him who claimed not to be what he was sure he must be. He said, more to himself than to the other, "But it makes sense. This is the area he was from. I only met you once, but the similarity is too strong. You're Frank's brother, just slightly changed in appearance, but still him."

"Master of Disguises, eh? 'Man of a Thousand Faces'? Like Lon Chaney?"

"Who?"

"Jesus, my friend. Your ignorance astounds me. One of the great silent film actors. 'Phantom of the Opera'? 'Hunchback of Notre Dame'? Could convincingly portray any variety of characters using only his makeup kit and his own God-given talent. Quite an innovator in his day. So you think I'm like him? Hell, with a little shoe polish maybe I could play even you."

"I could swear it was you. . . " Malcolm continued to examine the man through slit eyes, paying scarce attention to what he was saying.

"Well," the man said with finality, "I ain't. And now if you don't mind, I've got a set to finish."

He returned his attention to the keyboard and began another song.

Abashed, Malcolm stepped away into the shadows, walking backward, still watching the man at the piano. He sat back into a chair at an unoccupied table where he remained in a stunned and confused silence for an indiscernible moment of time. The piano player moved seamlessly from one song to the next, filling the room with melodies that, to Malcolm's ears, seemed increasingly infused with strident and dissonant atonalities. His eyes did not once look up to meet Malcolm's. When the waitress approached and asked for his order, Malcolm took no notice, but she politely repeated the question and, startled out of his trance, he ordered another bourbon. She returned a minute later with the drink and set it before him. It was then that he noticed that the room around him had emptied considerably. The din of many overlapping conversations that had previously filled the room was now almost completely absent, giving way to the ever-rising intensity and volume of the piano music as it climaxed to a resounding crescendo, followed by a sudden halt, a pause, and then ended with a final punctuating chord that signaled the conclusion of the set.

Jack the Piano Man got up from his seat and brushed off the front of his suit. The few remaining patrons in the restaurant clapped half-heartedly and left. Seeing that Malcolm remained at his table, the piano man ambled in his direction and sat down in the chair beside him as Malcolm followed his movement with his eyes.

"I'm sorry I brushed you off earlier—what'd you say your name was?"

"Malcolm."

"Uh, yeah, Malcolm. That was a bit rude. So, tell you what. I'll buy you a drink and we'll discuss this little dilemma of yours for a few minutes, alright? See if I can help you out any."

He smiled warmly and, before Malcolm could respond, indicated to the waitress for two more bourbons to be brought over.

"So!" he said cheerfully after the drinks had been brought. "What's on your mind? You say you're looking for your friend's brother?"

"Frank." Malcolm heard a weariness in his own voice that sounded new. "Frank was a friend of mine in Ohio. His brother Jonathan came to visit him last November, from New Jersey. From around here. Jersey City I think. Looked very much like you. They hadn't seen each other for many, many years. I and some others met Jonathan when he was there. A few days later Frank died very strangely—they called it a suicide. Jonathan mysteriously disappeared at the same time. Turns out this dude now really wasn't Frank's brother, because the real Jonathan was actually here in New Jersey at the time. But look, you already know all this because you're the one that was there, pretending to be Jonathan. I'm right, aren't I?"

"Offhand I'd say no. I don't know any of these characters you mention, friend, and I don't know you. And while other men might take great offense to what I think you are implying, I—" he lifted his glass and swallowed half his drink in one gulp, "—am a bigger man than that." He set his glass on the table and dabbed his mouth with a napkin.

Malcolm leaned forward and stared deep into the other's eyes. "What's your name?"

"I told you. Jack the Piano Man. Everyone here knows that. Of course, you could demand to see my ID, driver's license, something like that, but then you have no justification for harassing me in such a way, do you? And I'd have to complain to the hotel management, maybe even get the police involved. . . "

Malcolm's frustration began to grow, and he decided to abandon this line of inquiry and aim straight into the certainty that was now taking shape within his mind.

"What you did was wrong, man. Don't you see that?"

The other man shifted uncomfortably, looked to the distance, momentarily lost in thought. His presence seemed to alter slightly as he resumed speaking. "There is an unchangeable order to the universe. There must be." He looked back at Malcolm. "Fourier said that. Joseph Fourier. Physicist to Napoleon. . . mathematically described the distribution of heat through metals. Even discovered the greenhouse effect. . . " He paused to allow Malcolm to respond, which he did not, only staring hard and frowning at the other. "Anyway," he resumed, "Fourier claimed that if such a universal order could be grasped by our senses, it would produce a sensation comparable to that. . . of music." He smiled.

"How the hell does—"

"Of music!" He leaned forward, eyes wide with excitement. "The universe is musical! It's got a mainline straight into the emotional centers of the human brain. Therefore, nature is emotive. You see? It has to be that way. It can't just be some cold cosmic gulag. It has to be driven by feeling, by sensibility, by consciousness. By *our* consciousness. Otherwise there's no beauty. There's nothing."

"I don't know that I agree with you on that. What I do know is Frank's dead. Because of you. I don't care a damn about your philosophy, Mister—whoever you are—and I'm not interested in understanding your motives. He's dead. I don't know if you drove him to it—or worse. But you can't justify what you've done with a lot of fancy wordplay."

"I did nothing. Frank's death, well, let's call that a tragedy, because we choose to put such labels on things. Just as you're putting a label on me, Malcolm. You're attempting to make me out as something I'm not." He leaned forward meaningfully. "You see, friend, the fact is, I was never there. I've never been to your little Christian community. I've never been the privileged guest of the late, esteemed Frank What's-his-name."

"I *know* you were there. I saw you. *We* saw you."

"Can you prove it?"

They looked at each other for a moment. It was a deep look, full of unsaid meaning. Malcolm wondered if indeed he could.

Finally, the man spoke. "You know what Shakespeare's greatest tragedy was? Probably the greatest tragic story of all time? *Macbeth*. Why? Because all the misfortune visited upon Macbeth was brought about by himself, and it was completely unnecessary. Here was a guy—an intelligent, thoughtful guy—who had all the advantages. He was Thane of Glamis, which was not a bad gig. Then the King made him Thane of Cawdor, an even better position. He had everything going for him, yet he allowed his own ambition, his desire to be King of Scotland himself, to drive him into bad decisions which brought his downfall. It didn't have to happen that way, but he caused it to be. For my money, that's the purest definition of Tragedy. When we bring about our own destruction through our foolhardiness, even though all circumstances are in our favor. That's Macbeth." He leaned back and waved his hand in a gesture of pontification. "Now some might point to Hamlet as the greatest tragic hero, but he had little choice in his actions. He *had* to avenge his father. Romeo and Juliet—they had their families working against them. Lear had his deceitful daughters. These characters all had outside influences driving their behavior. But Macbeth," he paused and leaned forward again, "had only himself to blame. He had no excuse. Sure, his wife egged him on to kill the King, but the ease with which he caves in to her pressure, and the ease with which he follows one murder with many more, shows us that he and his wife were already of like mind before she even began to work on him." He leaned back in his chair. "Frank, at least as you describe him, was a tragic figure. His bad luck was his own fault, even though he had all the advantages. I ask you, why should we feel sorry for such a person?"

Malcolm could only narrow his eyes and shake his head incredulously. "You're a cold mother—"

"I'm cold? It's not I that's cold. Look around you. The world is cold. There is no moral center. Nature is not moral. Morality's a human construct."

Malcolm started and his eyes narrowed further. His voice was a whisper. "That's what he said."

"And the greatest universal tragedy is the fate of the human species, don't you think?" he continued as if he had not heard. "Here we are, the most intelligent life form ever evolved, with apparently unlimited potential. Millions of years of evolution have resulted in what we are today, an animal that can solve some of the most abstract mysteries of the universe, that has far more self-awareness than any other, and the emotional capacity to finally uncover and describe that musical order of the universe that brings about true beauty, that can actually bring about a moral center to an amoral cosmos—all these advantages we have. We have the knowledge to live in harmony

with each other and with nature, and the means to do it. We can
save ourselves from destruction—we know how. And what do
we do? We continue on our stupid, greedy, thoughtless path
toward exploding population growth, warfare, raping Mother
Earth with abandon—immediate gratification with no thought
for the consequences. That, my friend, is Tragedy—the greatest
of all tragedies. And you're not above it yourself. You're no
different than me."

Malcolm's impatience became manifest. "Enough of
this. All this jibber-jabber is very deep. I may even accept the
truth of some of it. But let me tell you something I don't think
you know. If you're really not who you claim not to be, this
won't matter to you much anyway. But the fact is, Frank had
a lot of money. He never told anyone, except for his next-door
neighbor. He may even have lied about it to this person who
visited him last November, whether it really was his brother or
not. Perhaps he was not and Frank had some suspicions about
him, which would be a good reason to lie to him. Anyway,
Frank's will stated that the bulk of this money should go to his
brother Jonathan. In fact, he changed it just before he died to
make it that way. So when Frank died, Jonathan became a pretty
rich man. But then the circumstances surrounding Frank's death
sort of clouded things, because it became questionable whether
Jonathan—or some person passing as him—had something
to do with Frank's death. In other words, it wasn't clear that
Frank's death wasn't helped along by someone who may have
benefited financially from his death. Then Jonathan himself died
before the questions were resolved. Now, we don't know, but
it's possible that Jonathan's will may specify that everything
he had should go to his ex-wife Ruth. That would include
everything he stood to gain from Frank's will. Ruth could stand
to become pretty wealthy once everything gets sorted out, once
the dead, as it were, are restored to their inheritance."

He paused and leaned forward, eyes riveted and level

with those of the placid face across from him. "If you are who I think you are, your old girlfriend is probably going to come into a heap of money. But you've got a problem now, bro, because the best way to assure that she gets her due is for you to 'fess up to what you did. So you got to ask yourself—how much are you willing to sacrifice for her? How much do you really love her? Mr. Reese Hart—and that's who you are, I'm certain of it now—don't you think that's worth it to set the musical order of the universe right?

"You see, I don't know that I disagree with you about your whole order-of-the-universe groove. You're probably right, but you're overreaching for justification of your actions. The universe *is* a cold place. I think you really know that as well as I do. The difference between you and me is, I've just kind of learned to accept it as such. But maybe as you say there is some underlying music to it that we just need to tap into, through our consciousness, our feeling. I know I sort of feel that when I get lost in some real good jazz. But I don't know one way or the other, and I don't really worry about it. I just live here in this little world. And I know that it can be pretty cold too. I surely have seen it. But it's all we can do to try to make things right *here*, in our little spheres of influence. And if we don't even do that, then all our complaining about the big cold universe is just a diversion. If we're not true and honest and loving within the small circle of life that we each inhabit, then we deserve to be insignificant. And if money's what drives you, man, then go ahead and live for that. But if that's where your high-flown ideals guide you, then pursue it out of love, not selfishness. See that people get their due. That's where the beauty you're craving comes from. Through your own actions.

"Now I think you're right about the human race. We're all doomed, because we're all fools. But know that that includes you as well. And know that there is no excuse for separating yourself from humanity. If anything it means we got to engage with each other all the more. Others depend on us; our future depends on us. We're at least intelligent enough to see that."

The other man, who had been emotionlessly following Malcolm's tirade, now smiled. "Oh yes, there's intelligence enough to go around. But what we're lacking is wisdom. Let's take you, for example. Now I'm going to tell you something you didn't know. You call me a liar. Well, maybe I am and maybe I ain't. I'm not even going to dignify that accusation with a defense. But there's something you may not know—you're a liar too. You're lying right now, in fact. To yourself. You've convinced yourself you're doing what's good and right. But are you? Whose ideals are you fulfilling? Who are you working for, Malcolm?"

Malcolm was jolted into realization as Ruth's last words to him, called out as he hastily retreated from her house, echoed in his brain. *Yes, who am I working for?* he wondered.

The other man leaned back in his chair and stared coldly, unsmilingly, into Malcolm's astonished eyes.

"Use your *wisdom*, Mr. Peters," he said, "not just your intelligence. You can't make the world perfect. Sometimes you have to just let it go."

Suddenly, Malcolm was feeling very tired. "Who are you, really?"

But the other simply shook his head, slowly, his face a façade of serious deliberation. "No," he said. "No, Malcolm. You won't get your way. The world won't let you." A relaxed smile slowly curled his lips. He rose from his seat and left a bill on the table to pay for the drinks. "We all have our destinies to fulfill, Mr. Peters. You have yours, and right now," he slid his chair under the table, "I must hasten to mine. Goodbye."

CHAPTER TWENTY-THREE

"It's time to wake up, Malcolm."

"Yes, yes, I know, Anna. Just give me a minute."

He woke with a start and found his unfamiliar surroundings lit with a diffuse, vapid light filtering in from behind the closed heavy drapes of the window. The light was white, vaguely fog-enshrouded, and by the brightness of the illumination it appeared to be late in the morning, much later than his usual rising time. Then he remembered—he was in a hotel room in Weehawken, New Jersey. He could not for the life of him recall how he ended up in the room. His last memory was sitting with that peculiar piano player in the deserted lounge with the red lights, feeling a little disoriented from too much drink and a conversation that skirted the outer boundaries of lucid reasoning, as he normally understood such things. But now he was lying in bed with his shoes off, his clothes still on and the covers pulled carelessly over him—and a gap in his memory that was unaccounted for.

"That cat was just plain bothersome," he exhaled as he swung his legs around the side of the bed and rubbed his hand over his head. He paused and stared at the floor.

And now he was dreaming of Anna again. *She seems to always talk to me in my sleep. Like she thinks that's the only time when I won't be so quick to push her away with my so-called 'rational thinking'—tell her that she can't really be there.*

He stood and looked in the large mirror above the dresser. He was surprised to see that his reflection appeared much healthier this morning than he would have expected, indeed better than he remembered it being even last night. His features seemed more defined and focused, and turning his inspection inward he found his mood exhibited the freshness of one recently reborn.

He searched around for his overnight bag. *Well, if she is talking to me, she's telling me I better get going. I have to check out by noon, then catch a plane tonight in Newark.*

Malcolm checked the time, then took a quick shower, put on some fresh clothes, and packed his belongings. He left a tip for the maid on the nightstand, took up his coat and suitcase, and vacated the room. At the registration desk in the lobby, he turned in his room key and settled his bill. He had plenty of time before his flight from Newark that evening, and decided that a walk around the town would be a sensible means by which to pass the afternoon hours. Suitcase in hand, he strolled through the brass-framed revolving front door, gave a nod to the smartly dressed doorman, explained that he would return later to engage a cab to the airport, and descended the marble steps to the sidewalk. The early afternoon was clouded over, subtly warm but tinged with the chill of lingering late winter, the air feeling poised on the cusp of its impending transition to very early spring. He strode along the bustling streets purposelessly, exhibiting a wandering curiosity in the sights around him: the crawling automobile traffic speaking in clipped, punctuated horn blasts; the pedestrian-crowded sidewalks and storefronts; the squat grimness of the surrounding architecture; the contrasting panoramic backdrop of the gray flowing Hudson and, on its distant shore, the encroaching Manhattan skyline.

On he walked, slowly, unthinkingly, unaware of time or place. He traveled in circles without realizing it, stopped to look vacantly into storefronts and down empty alleyways. The afternoon crawled past and began to fade before he knew it. Eventually, he found himself ascending a hill as he walked, leaving behind the downtown center, moving up Kennedy Boulevard, past the entrance to the Lincoln Tunnel, under the 495 overpass, then climbing toward a promontory that overlooked Port Imperial Boulevard and offered a view of the lights defining the waterfront below. Malcolm had now entered upon a neighborhood of handsome, hedge-lined houses that looked out beyond a picturesque little tree-dotted but leafless park and across the river to the forbidding city skyscrapers. He followed a path along the sidewalk between the road and the edge of the park, feeling drawn to an area where the walkway was lined with a low iron fence. Set off slightly from the path, enclosed and isolated by its own square of low fencing, stood a shadowed bronze bust atop a shoulder-high white stone pedestal. He paused. He could almost feel the moisture-laden echoes pulsating from the labyrinthine tunnels and underground chambers permeating the solid Palisades sill below him. Slowly he approached the bust, staring at it, watching it emerge into focus from out of the foggy grayness surrounding it. He could see the face now, could almost place it. He looked down. At the base of the pedestal was a brownish boulder upon the surface of which, when he circled round to the back of the monument, was revealed to have been chiseled an inscription. He leaned over and read, with the lights of New York City behind him:

"UPON THIS STONE RESTED THE HEAD OF PATRIOT, SOLDIER, STATESMAN, AND JURIST ALEXANDER HAMILTON, AFTER THE DUEL WITH AARON BURR."

Yes, of course. Now he remembered. Below him was the spot where the infamous duel occurred between the Treasury Secretary and the Vice President in 1804, political rivals squaring off at the foot of the Palisades cliffs facing the Hudson River on the New Jersey side one warm July morning. It had been the ridiculous end of a man of great achievement and promise, all for the sake of some childish argument over honor and ambition, or some such. A ridiculous death, much—Malcolm remembered with a startled flash—much like the ridiculous death of Frank Allerton. What brought that to mind? he wondered. Ridiculous Death. But then, he considered, all death was ridiculous. There was no such thing as a dignified death, despite all marketing to the contrary. Does the dying impala say, "My but this is a glorified way to go" as the lion claws it to the ground, shredded and dripping and crusted over with sand, and proceeds to chomp it into greasy, gore-soaked pieces? Or does it simply whimper to itself, with no hope of salvation, declaring "What a ridiculous end"? Did Jesus not think the same thing, hanging naked and vanquished with nails through his wrists and feet and blood congealing in his eyes, crying his eternal "why?" to the heavens? What of the millions of battle-dead, or the earthquake, hurricane, avalanche, plane crash, murder, and bridge-collapse dead, or the casualties of the slow, relentless march of disease, of time and exhaustion? Are not the final exits of both the great and the not-so-great characterized by qualities of equal absurdity when viewed with cold, hard, distant dispassion? Surely Anna's death, he recalled, was not punctuated by pretensions at dignity. She made no claim to such fakery in that regard. All we are, all we have been spending our entire lives defining and delineating about ourselves, becomes collapsed and sucked into the pinpoint vortex of deliberate, malevolent, unyielding extermination at that last moment. There is no place for pride in these circumstances. Do the leaders of collapsing empires not view their demises as ludicrous as well? It was all part of the unlimited human capacity for the preposterous. So it was for the great Hamilton. And for his role in the calamity, Burr was never prosecuted. So it goes.

Malcolm straightened and stood looking around him at the now fading, twilit park, sensing his isolation. Below him, the lights of the waterfront gave off a silent, heatless glow; the few boats on the river glided placidly by, barely visible, some illuminated by red and white lights. He felt oddly at home here, despite his feeling of aloneness. He looked up to the vertical skyscraper lights of far-off Manhattan. *I mean, they had warnings, right?* He remembered having said that, the night at the Colonel's house, the last time he saw Frank alive.

With a sudden awakening he remembered his appointed flight, held up his wristwatch to squint at its dial under the dispersed streetlamp illumination. He needed to head back to the hotel, to follow up on one last thread of investigation before catching a cab to the airport. He snatched up his suitcase, turned and walked swiftly down the misty sidewalks, retracing the route he had followed to reach the overlook. He began to sweat slightly with the exertion, stepping quickly and feeling weighed down by his grip, which he occasionally switched from one hand to the other. All the while he was thinking of his encounter the previous night, the encounter with the piano player, and the dissatisfied feeling with which the whole affair had left him. He wanted to go back there one last time before he departed, to see what more he could find out.

Back at the hotel, he trotted up the marble steps and entered through the revolving door into the hushed lobby, then immediately turned right to go into the restaurant. It was a little past five o'clock and there were small groups of dinner patrons at the tables, but the bar was only sparsely populated. He approached a clear space where the bartender was busily wiping a rag over the varnished surface of the dark wood with his head down. Malcolm spoke quickly to the man before being acknowledged, feeling pressed for time.

"The piano player you have here—he'll be back tonight?"

The man continued wiping down the bar and said without looking up, "Not so far as I know. My manager told me he quit last night."

"Quit?"

"Yeah. Some family emergency. Brother died suddenly, I think he said. So he just quit and left town. Collected his pay and left. Said he wouldn't be back."

Malcolm stood there and pondered this, watching the concentric circular motions the rag made on the bar as the man continued his work. Finally he asked, "Do you know what his name was?"

The man stopped wiping the bar and tossed the rag in a bin behind him. He faced Malcolm and stood with both hands on the bar, staring off in the distance, concentrating on the question.

"Jack somebody," he said, then shrugged his shoulders. "I dunno. I didn't really pay attention to 'im. He'd come in a few nights a week for the past year or so. I never really got to know 'im."

Malcolm picked up his suitcase and left the restaurant, then exited the hotel through the brass-framed revolving door and paused on the marble steps. At his request, the smartly dressed doorman summoned a cab and Malcolm descended the steps and stooped to get in the car. "Newark Airport," he said as the door closed beside him.

The taxi merged into traffic and Malcolm rolled down his window slightly. Dusk was fully unfolding as they drove out of town to the turnpike and entered upon pock-marked concrete causeways layered over garbage-strewn marshland with water the color of oil and grasses the color of straw. In the distance, the industrial terrain stood silent and looming, sprinkled with scattered flocks of waterfowl soaring past monolithic brick buildings and rust-encrusted smokestacks. He watched the endless, indifferent streams of cars and trucks traversing the jumble of raised highways in tedious motion like corpuscles pulsing through a cadaver. His was one of many vehicles navigating a vast warren spread across a darkening vista of decay.

At the airport, Malcolm checked in, obtained his boarding pass, and moved through security without incident. When he boarded the plane, he found his seat by the window just behind the wing. He excused himself as he stepped past the passenger already seated by the aisle, an earnest looking young man of about twenty, busily text-messaging on his cell phone. When Malcolm got settled, the young man turned to him and smiled seriously. "How's it going?" he said.

Malcolm nodded. "Pretty good. You?"

"Alright. Headin' back home to Pittsburgh for a few days." He finished his message and turned off the cell phone, stuffed it in his shirt pocket.

They sat in silence while the crew prepared for take-off and the plane taxied out onto the runway. After a pause, the giant behemoth accelerated, gained speed rapidly with a whir of engines, and finally lifted gently into the air. Malcolm looked out the window to take in one last time the endless prospect of the New Jersey lights below him. When they finally reached cruising altitude, he lay back in his seat and closed his eyes.

The young man next to him spoke suddenly, loudly, so as to be heard over the engine roar. "You live in Pittsburgh?"

Malcolm opened his eyes and raised his head, turning. "Uh, no. Ohio."

Oblivious to any consideration that he might be disturbing his neighbor, the young man continued, leaning toward Malcolm and speaking at full volume, "I'm going back home for a few days. Pittsburgh. North Fayette. We're having a party for my older brother. He's getting ready to head out to Iraq."

"Oh, I'm sorry to hear that."

"Oh, no, it's not so bad. I'm mean, he's glad to do it. We're all glad. My family's real proud of him, believe it or not. I'd like to join up too, but I gotta finish business school first."

"Well, you've got to maintain your priorities."

"And also follow the courage of your convictions, don't you think?" He stared intently at Malcolm. "There's not enough people now who do that. I mean, who take a stand and really stick to it. Who know what's right and what's wrong, and really follow through on their beliefs."

Malcolm did not feel like arguing at the moment, but was unable to suppress his innate tendency to play the role of pedagogue. He felt like he'd had this conversation before. "Well, other people may feel just as committed to their own beliefs as you do to yours. Their beliefs just happen to be different."

"I don't have a problem with people having different beliefs. It's just when they start imposing them on the rest of us—telling us how to think, how to act—that's where I draw the line. Like the ones in charge now—" he gave Malcolm a wry smile, "—I'm not gonna name any names. But what they're doing to our country—I don't mean any disrespect, mind you, but we are in serious danger of having our freedoms taken away, believe it or not."

"How so?"

"Well, it's kind of like Nazi Germany, isn't it? It was all perfectly legal, what they did. And they were just slowly chiseling away, chipping away at people's liberties, so slowly that the people hardly noticed. Then one day you wake up and you're a prisoner in your own country, with no rights whatsoever. No right to exercise your religious beliefs, to spend your money how you want, to say what you want. And it's all been done right under our noses, perfectly legal. I mean, I read. I watch the news. You know, we're not all fools in this country."

"No, I expect not."

"The government's way out of control. They're leading us in a direction that abandons the principles this country was founded on. In a few years we'll be a socialist state, spreading the wealth everywhere, and then what will the citizens of this country have left? What defense will we have against those who want to destroy our way of life? I'm still young. I don't want my freedoms taken away. Believe it or not, there's still a few of us who are willing to fight back. Just wait and see. . . "

The young man talked on, overcome with garrulous passion, paying little mind to the fact that Malcolm's attention was fading. After a few minutes, he exhausted himself, saw that Malcolm had ceased to be responsive, and sat back in his seat gently nodding his head in affirmation of his justified righteous indignation. Malcolm, for his part, took the opportunity to try sleep, dozed a few times, but never found a deep, restful slumber. His mind was too edgy and agitated right now. Finally, he resigned himself to the fact that he was fully awake, and would remain so for the duration of his flight. He stared out the window at the blinking red lights that lined the rear edge of the jet's wing—lights that seemed to draw him in slowly, hypnotically, into a waking dream, or perhaps an unyielding trance, a state of new and saddened awareness that he knew would remain, obstinate, never to leave him.

CHAPTER TWENTY-FOUR

He was in a car. Or perhaps a train. No—a car. There was a road ahead, an empty road, visible in the headlights. All around, darkness. And the sound of a motor running. And a sensation of forward movement, a jostling of his body within the confines of a seat belt. His head lolled to the side and back again.

He heard a low moan—immediately realized it was his own. In the corner of his blurred vision, he thought he saw a woman—the driver, perhaps—turn her head toward him then back to the road ahead. *Is this another mad dream?*

He tried to remember, had a vague recollection of a party—or was it a celebration?—with another person. *My wife?* Yes, it was Ruth. A celebration of sorts in a comfortable living room at night. He was sitting in a brown armchair facing a warm fire in the hearth. She'd entered the room with something in each hand. Two glasses of champagne. *I'm sure it will work out fine*, she was saying. *I don't see why not. You've packed your bag?* she asked. *By the front door, babe.* He was speaking now. *But why can't we stay here?* She gave him an indulgent smile. *Don't be silly. You know it's better this way with him still poking around. Anyway, it will all resolve itself in a few days, then you and I can begin again.* She handed him a glass, sat upon the padded arm of his chair and held up her own glass. *Let's toast—to us.* They clinked glasses. He raised his own drink to his lips. *Yeah babe, to us. No more living like a chump. Let's drink to it. I almost thought it wouldn't happen. That old joker really blindsided me at first. But I guess we lucked out.* She was almost laughing now. *I can't believe you actually did that. You always were a crazy fool.* He was laughing too. *Well, it came together in the end, didn't it? For a while there I'd thought you'd sold me out, were telling stories behind my back. I never could trust you, babe. Guess that's why I can't resist you. And aren't you glad I was there for you when hubby croaked? After you swore you never wanted to see me again.* She leaned her face into his. *Well, you're hard to keep away, darling.* She kissed him. Then she was in his arms, caressing him, her hands sliding along his shirt fabric, pressing upon the sweat permeating his skin. *But tell me, doll,* he was saying, *was it you who put the cops on his trail? Was that your doing? So smart of you, but it was smarter than even you could have imagined. Who'da known it would kill him?* She pressed her lips again to his as she pulled him up from the chair and gently began to push him back toward the front door. *Shut up, tiger. No need to talk it to death. Besides, we have to get ready.* He was being pushed backward, feeling a little light in the head now. *But I still don't see why we need to rush out—* he stumbled slightly, almost fell back on the floor. Suddenly the room was spinning around him.

Whoah! Ruth I'm real tired now. I—

Are you darling? Feeling alright? A little exhausted, dear? I'm not surprised. Here. Give me your glass. Darling? Can you hear me? Jake? Jake dear? Let's go to the car. We'll drive around for a while. The cool air will do you good. Come on darling. I've got your coat right here. Out the door. Down the steps. Now get in the car. There you go. I'll go back for your bag. Don't worry. Are you feeling better? Can you hear me darling? Jake? Jake? Can you hear me?

The car seemed to be slowing—descending on a gravel road through the pitch black darkness. The headlights revealed through his half-open eyes a brief glimpse of a clearing as the car turned. The lights swept past a few abandoned buildings, long tables scattered about, storage sheds shut tight. *They closed for the winter I see.* Then the car headed toward what looked like a small beach and a serene, wide black lake. They approached the water at a slow crawl now. He saw a rowboat settled in the shallows by the shore. *This looks familiar.* The car came to a halt and the headlights extinguished suddenly, then the engine stopped. Total darkness now. He closed his eyes and felt like going back to sleep. He heard a car door opening and slamming shut. Then another opening, this one closer to him. No sounds. No wait, that's not true. He heard the gentle lapping of tiny waves on the shore. And he felt cold air, then a heavy pull on his body. *Let's take the boat,* she was saying. He heard grunting, felt a sensation of being roughly handled, followed by a painful slamming of his shin against hard wood. *Ouch!* He was lying down on a hard floor, uncomfortably. But it felt good to lie down. He wanted to sleep. In his slumber he heard the sound of splashing water, soothing and rhythmic. Slow, gliding movement, almost like he was flying. *What a beautiful night. No stars. No moonlight. But I'm a little chilled. . .*

     He felt gentle rocking and cold against his skin, heard the chinking sounds of thick metal pieces sliding over themselves. *It's so heavy. What is that? Feels almost like chains.* A sudden realization. *Ruth? Are you sleeping too? Do you hear that? It's all right now Ruth. It's all over. We'll be fine. Why are you shoving? Roll over and go back to sleep.*

     A splashing sound, loud and jarring. Suddenly cold. And wet. *It's raining Ruth. We'd better get inside. My feet are wet.* He laughed. *I'm falling out of the bed!* More splashing. *Ruth it's a downpour. I'm soaked.*

     Then a gurgle. A coughing, choking gurgle.

     Ruth there's a leak in the roof. It's pouring into my mouth.

     He opened his eyes and caught a glimpse of her face in the sky, looking down through the ceiling.

     Why are you up there? But it's dark now. So hard to see. Ruth you're getting blurry. I'm soaked now. And very cold. Why is it so cold?

A hollow deep sound filled his ears, then no sound at all. Water everywhere. . .

Ruth I can't breathe!

Falling.

Ruth you're moving away. The floor's sinking. Come back! My God it's cold. Ruth I can't hear you! There's no air!

Oh Jesus it's dark. I can't wake up! Ruth! Ruth!. . .

CHAPTER TWENTY-FIVE

In the Sunnyland Diner, a week hence, Malcolm and Gretchen sat in a booth by the window facing out onto the main street with its parade of cars and pedestrians giving a semblance of life to the otherwise dead surroundings. The afternoon, as Malcolm would later recall, was passing like the panels of a slide show, one episode fading as another emerged. Scenes watched through the window provided little indication that time was progressing. It was almost as if people moved in an endless cycle of repetition, like the figures in the Wilmot cuckoo clock, as he, feeling wrecked and overpowered, cheerlessly related the events of his brief expedition to New Jersey in search of an elusive answer that remained beyond reach. It was a pitiable denouement, an anti-climactic coda with which he ended his journey.

"It was not what I expected," he concluded in a disheartened tone, "and I can't say that I was satisfied with the outcome."

Gretchen eyed him curiously over her coffee cup.

"So the police," he was saying, "have established to their satisfaction that Jonathon Allerton was not in town at the time of Frank's death—in fact, they have no evidence he was here at any time before Frank died. His ex-wife sticks to her story about Jonathan's whereabouts when Frank died, as well as denying any knowledge that he drove out here several weeks before, in spite of what she told me, and they have no evidence to dispute that. Therefore, there is no reason to hold up the execution of the wills, in the minds of the authorities. Colonel Haygood came back from Florida to take care of it. I just spoke with him yesterday. Frank's money will mostly go to Jonathon's estate, and—you were right—Jonathan's will leaves everything in turn to the ex. She'll be very well off now. . . " He paused, sighed deeply and looked at Gretchen. "And I don't know how good I feel about that."

Anna would not be proud of him. No, he didn't do anything wrong; he just didn't do anything right. Although what he could have done to have changed things he did not know. Perhaps it was the effort wasted on an unsatisfactory result that bothered him more than the result itself. He might say he had done his best, but so what? Anna had always told him, one's good intentions may comfort the giver, but they do little for the recipient of a worthless gift. It's not the thought that counts; it's the action, and then the upshot. In this case his actions had proved useless, perhaps had even made things worse.

Gretchen seemed to be thinking of something else. She asked suddenly, "You know that prayer? 'God grant me the courage to change what I can, the serenity to accept what I can't change, and the wisdom to tell the difference'? Or something like that?"

"Right now I'd prefer not to know the difference." Malcolm stared out the window.

"As far as who that guy was who came here and claimed to be Frank's brother," he was saying, "well, I don't know. I really thought I had seen him playing piano at that hotel, but I can't be sure. It seems too coincidental. And the funny thing is, after I checked out the next day, I went into the restaurant and asked about the piano player. Well, the bartender said he'd been there for about a year, but that after he finished working the night before, he quit. Said he had a family emergency come up and he had to leave the area suddenly. He said his brother had died, of all things. Now isn't that curious? Who knows where he went or if he can even be traced again? He seems to have a number of identities, and apparently no one sees it as important enough to sort out just who he really is. He sort of just crawls in and out of the woodwork."

"Well, don't you want to follow up on this?" Gretchen asked. "You've put so much into it already."

Malcolm leaned back in the booth and rubbed his hand over his face, top to bottom, as if wiping away the sweat of past exertions, sighing as he did it. "Nah. I'm tired. I'm just tired of going over old ground. Maybe it's all for the best, anyway. I need to look ahead—move forward, you know? I gotta finish this kite I'm working on for my granddaughter. She'll be three next month, and I want to bring it up to her then. Just the right age to start to learn about flying."

It was a long and dreary late-winter afternoon. The pace of time remained slower than normal. Gretchen set her cup down in the saucer with a clink and raised her eyes to her companion.

"Malcolm, tell me about your son. I mean, what does he do in Youngstown?"

"Well, they're just outside of Youngstown. He's a contract lawyer. Been doing that for a number of years. Graduated fifth in his class from UDC Law School—that's the University of the District of Columbia."

"Oh."

"His wife Renee's a lawyer too. That's how they met. She set it aside when she got pregnant, but I think she wants to get back to practicing some as soon as the baby is old enough."

"Mm."

"He's been saying lately he wants to get into politics.

Maybe run for state legislature. Wouldn't that be something?"

"He must have inherited the political bug from you, huh? You used to take an interest in stuff like that, right?"

Malcolm smiled. "Yeah, a little."

Gretchen was pensive as she stared out the window at the bleak landscape, watched the crows foraging in the parking lot across the street. The afternoon was waning, beginning to darken. "It was unusually warm the other day," she said. "I'm hoping spring will be early this year."

"I don't know. The weather's turned cold again."

"Yeah." She turned her head and looked across the diner to Cora, who was taking orders at a table near the kitchen doors.

"Still, it doesn't seem right," she said. "Things like this shouldn't be allowed to happen without some consequences. It makes you wonder if there's such a thing as justice."

"Yeah, well. Sometimes there is and sometimes there isn't. And sometimes you let it go just to get by."

She turned back to him. "Let it go? Is that what we're being reduced to these days?"

Malcolm said nothing, just gazed out the window at the murky sky. He wondered if the answer even mattered to him anymore. *You set your sights on great things when you begin your life. You think you'll do great things, change the world in a big way. Be a part of it all. Idealist to the end, you tell yourself. But then the world doesn't allow much room for idealism. Or else maybe that alone just isn't enough. Maybe you do need a rock solid foundation in courage, and a real sense of conviction that doesn't allow for wavering. Not fanatical or dogmatic—just solid. . . and real. . . and right. I used to have that. What happened to it?*

Gretchen was speaking again. He turned and saw her looking at him. "It makes people do terrible things, doesn't it?" she was saying.

"Hmm? What's that?"

"Money. It makes people do terrible things to each other, just to get some more of it. Isn't that what happened here, with Frank's will and all? Wouldn't we be better off if people could just take care of each other without worrying about getting money?"

"Yeah, well, the world doesn't seem to work that way. Believe me, I've tried to figure out another way, but the system doesn't seem to allow it. Back in the day, money was invented as a tool for people to trade with. Now we're the tools of money. It doesn't seem like it's going to change anytime soon."

Gretchen nodded and sipped her coffee, looking distractedly at the table. Suddenly she brightened and reached for Malcolm's sleeve. "Oh, hey!" she exclaimed. "I forgot to tell you. My poem's going to be published! The one I showed you."

Malcolm looked up and said with genuine pleasure, "Well, that's great! Congratulations."

She smiled and blushed. "Thanks. It's just a little poetry magazine that probably nobody reads. But it's a start."

"Yes, it's a start." He regarded her in a way that made her think his mind had drifted elsewhere, to new horizons, maybe new possibilities. Then he said with hushed sincerity, "I'm real proud of you."

Within minutes, snow began falling. Gretchen stared at it through the window and sighed. "I guess spring won't be coming early after all." She turned her head back to Malcolm, who was watching her across the table. Then a wistful, yet knowing, expression overtook her features. She appeared to look into him with a determined intensity he had never before seen, an appearance of resolute and defiant satisfaction. He knew what she was going to say before she said it. "And that's fine too, isn't it?"